THE TEXAS TATTLER
All the news that's barely fit to print!

IT'S RAINING MEN...

Ladies, pack your bags and fur-lined parkas. While we've always heard that Alaskan men are hungry for a little female companionship to warm up those long, blustery cold nights, it appears that eligible males are now falling from the skies...literally!

At least that's how Fortune heiress Holly Douglas met bush pilot Guy Blackwolf. Seems he'd been hired by the Fortune family to bring the reluctant heiress back to Red Rock, when his plane encoutered some bad weather and crash-landed in a nearby lake. Fortunately, Holly was on the scene, and,

from the looks of Guy, she gave him plenty of tender loving care during his *long* recovery. Guy claims that all his wounds have healed, but he still seemed to be a bit dazed and reeling from more than a concussion when *The Tattler* spoke to him.

Has this pilot just met a force greater than even Mother Nature...Cupid?

Dear Reader,

Welcome to Silhouette Desire, where you can indulge yourself every month with six passionate, powerful and provocative romances! And you can take romance one step further.... Look inside for details about our exciting new contest, "Silhouette Makes You a Star."

Popular author Mary Lynn Baxter returns to Desire with our MAN OF THE MONTH when *The Millionaire Comes Home* to Texas to reunite with the woman he could never forget. Rising star Sheri WhiteFeather's latest story features a *Comanche Vow* that leads to a marriage of convenience...until passionate love transforms it into the real thing.

It's our pleasure to present you with a new miniseries entitled 20 AMBER COURT, featuring four twentysomething female friends who share an address...and their discoveries about life and love. Don't miss the launch title, *When Jayne Met Erik,* by beloved author Elizabeth Bevarly. The scandalous Desire miniseries FORTUNES OF TEXAS: THE LOST HEIRS continues with *Fortune's Secret Daughter* by Barbara McCauley. Alexandra Sellers offers you another sumptuous story in her miniseries SONS OF THE DESERT: THE SULTANS, *Sleeping with the Sultan.* And the talented Cindy Gerard brings you a touching love story about a man of honor pledged to marry an innocent young woman with a secret, in *The Bridal Arrangement.*

Treat yourself to all six of these tantalizing tales from Silhouette Desire.

Enjoy!

Joan Marlow Golan

Joan Marlow Golan
Senior Editor, Silhouette Desire

Please address questions and book requests to:
Silhouette Reader Service
U.S.: 3010 Walden Ave., P.O. Box 1325, Buffalo, NY 14269
Canadian: P.O. Box 609, Fort Erie, Ont. L2A 5X3

Fortune's Secret Daughter

BARBARA McCAULEY

Published by Silhouette Books

America's Publisher of Contemporary Romance

Special thanks and acknowledgment are given to Barbara McCauley for her contribution to the FORTUNES OF TEXAS: THE LOST HEIRS series.

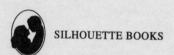 SILHOUETTE BOOKS

ISBN 0-373-76390-5

FORTUNE'S SECRET DAUGHTER

Copyright © 2001 by Harlequin Books S.A.

This edition published by arrangement with Harlequin Books S.A.

® and TM are trademarks of Harlequin Books S.A., used under license. Trademarks indicated with ® are registered in the United States Patent and Trademark Office, the Canadian Trade Marks Office and in other countries.

Visit Silhouette at www.eHarlequin.com

Printed in U.S.A.

BARBARA McCAULEY

was born and raised in California and has spent a good portion of her life exploring the mountains, beaches and deserts so abundant there. The youngest of five children, she grew up in a small house, and her only chance for a moment alone was to sneak into the backyard with a book and quietly hide away.

With two children of her own now and a busy household, she still finds herself slipping away to enjoy a good novel. A daydreamer and incurable romantic, she says writing has fulfilled her most incredible dream of all—breathing life into the people in her mind and making them real. She has one loud and demanding Amazon parrot named Fred and a German shepherd named Max. When she can manage the time, she loves to sink her hands into fresh-turned soil and make things grow.

THE FORTUNES OF TEXAS™

 Meet the Fortunes of Texas

Meet the Fortunes of Texas's Lost Heirs—membership in this Texas family has its privileges and its price. As the family gathers to welcome its newest members, it discovers a murderer in its midst...and passionate new romances that only a true-bred Texas love can bring!

CAST OF CHARACTERS

Holly Douglas: She thought she'd run as far away as she could from the Fortune family and the dusty-dry Texas trailer park where she'd grown up. But fate and the handsome stranger she'd just rescued had their own agendas....

Guy Blackwolf: Built solid as a western red cedar, this pilot had yet to meet a female who could get the better of him. And then he went head-to-head with Mother Nature...and Holly Douglas!

Jonas Goodfellow: The Fortunes had opened their homes to this lost heir, but had he repaid their generosity by poisoning the family patriarch?

One

The storm came on fast and hard, slapped at the tiny seaplane as if it were a pesky gnat instead of three thousand pounds of metal and man. Thunder boomed and a second assault on the plane tipped the nose dangerously downward. Metal groaned while the man swore, struggling to hold on to the wheel and stay in control.

"Come on, sweetheart, stay with me," Guy Black-wolf hissed through clenched teeth. "We've seen worse than this."

Thick clouds swallowed machine and man whole. A jagged bolt of lightning exploded not more than twenty feet from the plane's left wing, momentarily turning Guy's world a brilliant, blinding white. He blinked furiously, tightened his grip on the throttle and eased the plane's nose level while the wind rocked the wings like a child's teeter-totter.

"Steady, steady," he coaxed with the patience of a lover. "That's my girl."

He knew he was close. He could see the tops of the trees thirty feet below and according to his instruments, Twin Pines Lake was two hundred feet ahead. Two more minutes and he'd be safe and sound, gliding smoothly over the water to shore.

He could do it. He *would* do it. He owed a friend a favor, and he refused to let anything—not even a miserable storm in the wilderness of Alaska—get in his way. Mother Nature might be one tough broad, but Guy Blackwolf had yet to meet a female that he'd let get the better of him.

The storm opened up like the jaws of a giant beast and closed around the plane, then gave a savage shake. The throttle shook fiercely under Guy's hand, but he held firm, eyes narrowed, jaw tight. Just another hundred feet. Piece of cake, he told himself as he eased the plane down.

He gave a hoot of victory as he broke through the blanket of thick gray and the lake emerged below him. He spotted the dark blue Land Rover parked close to the north bank, knew that the woman was waiting for him. Well, not for *him,* he thought with a smile. She thought he was merely bringing supplies for her store. He'd let her keep thinking that, until he assessed the situation. She wasn't going to like it, but when the moment was right, he'd tell her who he really was, and why he'd come.

He caught sight of the woman standing close to the

shore, though he couldn't make out her features or see her hair under the rain slicker she wore. He'd see soon enough, he thought and gently guided the plane lower.

Without warning, an explosion rocked the tail section of his plane and sent the machine into a downward tilt. Smoke filled the cockpit and the scent of burning metal choked the air. Guy swore hotly and frantically struggled with the controls. But it was no good.

He was going down, and there wasn't a damn thing he could do about it.

Holly Douglas stared hard over the tops of the spruce trees, searching for the plane that she could hear, but couldn't see. The storm had rolled in expectedly, one of those summer occurrences that were frequent enough to keep the land green and lush and the lake high, but not so frequent as to slow down anyone who lived here. Of all the things that the twelve hundred residents of Twin Pines didn't need, it was to slow down. Life here moved at its own calm, steady pace.

At the sound of the approaching plane, Holly frowned. The rain had started to come down harder, pelting her slicker and sliding down the shiny yellow fabric. She winced at the flash of lightning from the south, then frowned. Definitely not a day to be out flying. Special order supplies came in on seaplanes every two weeks via Pelican Pilots, a Seattle-based company Holly had been using since she'd bought the general store three years ago. She even knew all the pilots by name.

Suddenly the plane shot out of the clouds in a downward spiral, engine sputtering and tail end smoking. It rose, then swept down again, heading straight for the lake. Horrified, Holly watched as the pilot managed to lift the nose at the last moment, but not enough to avoid a collision. The scream of ripping metal split the air as the plane bounced once off the water, then again before coming to a stop twenty feet from shore.

Heart pounding, Holly had her slicker off in two seconds, then her boots. She dived into the lake, gasped at the slap of frigid water and was at the plane in ten strong strokes. She yanked open the pilot's door as the plane tipped dangerously on its side, threatening to suck man and machine under.

His hair was coal-black, one thick shock on his forehead matted with blood that streamed from a cut on his temple. Dazed, he grappled with his seat belt, but couldn't seem to unbuckle himself.

"I've got it," Holly yelled over the still sputtering engine and the boom of rolling thunder.

As she pulled herself up, he glanced at her with eyes as gray as the storm overhead. In one fluid movement, she brushed the man's hands out of the way and had him unbuckled. None too gently, she grabbed him by the shirt collar and dragged him out of the smoking plane. He fell with a limp splash into the cold water, sputtered, then flung his arms weakly.

"Be still," she yelled again and took off for shore, one hand tightly clutching the collar of his navy-blue shirt while she kicked her way back to land. He was tall and lean, built solid as a lumberjack, but in the water he floated behind her like a piece of thick driftwood.

She stumbled onto shore a few seconds later and dragged the pilot up onto the grassy bank. Out of the water he was a good two hundred pounds plus wet clothes and boots and she had to strain to pull him free of the lake. Gasping for breath, Holly fell to her knees beside the man. Rain pelted them, and she knew she had to get him out of the elements and into her Land Rover.

"Are you hurt?" she shouted over the storm.

His eyes were open, but glazed over and she wasn't sure if he'd heard her. Blood still oozed from the gash on his temple, mixing with the rain as it ran down his face. She quickly ran her hands over his body, checking for broken bones or serious injuries. Lightning ripped through the thick clouds and struck not fifty feet away.

"We've got to get you into my car," she yelled. "Can you walk?"

He nodded weakly, then rose on an elbow and nearly fell back again, but she caught him under the arm and braced her body against his. He stumbled to his knees, then stood on wobbly legs. Looping his arm around her shoulders, they staggered the few feet to the car and she yanked open the back seat door, then eased him onto the seat. They were both shivering from the wet and cold, and she reached for a wool blanket from behind the seat and tossed it over him.

"Hang on." She tucked the edges of the blanket under him. "I'll get you to Doc right away."

"My plane," he muttered faintly as he struggled to rise.

"Later." She placed a hand on his arm to ease him back down. "Let's just worry about you right now."

He mumbled something unintelligible, then fell back onto the seat. His head rolled to one side and his eyes closed.

Teeth chattering, Holly jumped in the driver's seat. She prayed the man's injuries didn't require a hospital. The closest one was fifty miles away. In this storm, it would take an hour and a half to get there. When the engine roared to life, she gunned it, spraying dirt and mud as she headed for the road back to town.

His first thought when he woke was that he'd kissed one too many shots of Quervo Gold at Manny's Cantina the night before: the pounding in his skull, the searing pulse in his eyeballs, the lack of cooperation from his arms and legs when he struggled to sit. All indications that he'd had one hell of an evening at the bar where he spent most Friday nights. A fresh bolt of pain sliced his brain in half when he moved his head, and he gritted his teeth on a groan.

He really needed to find something else to do with his Friday nights, Guy thought. Something that didn't require a bottle of extra-strength aspirin and three pots of coffee when he woke up the next morning.

"Hey—" Guy froze at the sound of the distinctly feminine whisper close to his ear "—you awake?"

Uh-oh. He never mixed Friday night drinking with women. It was important to be clearheaded around the female gender at all times, Guy believed. Words could be misconstrued and twisted, and a night of pleasure could suddenly become extremely complicated. He was *always* careful when he spent the night with a woman. At least, he *had* always been careful.

Slowly, carefully, he opened his eyes.

It took a moment for his vision to clear and make out the woman's features. Delicate brows arched high over eyes the color of wild honey, the irises rimmed with a circle of dark brown. Her lashes were thick and long, the same deep shade of fire-brown as her wavy, shoulder-length hair. His gaze settled on her mouth and in spite of the pounding in his head, he couldn't help but admire the wide, soft lips only inches from his own. Her skin was smooth and pale, the narrow bridge of her straight nose sprinkled with freckles.

She smelled like…disinfectant?

Disinfectant? He frowned. Strange, but who was he to argue with a woman who liked to clean? If he'd really gotten lucky, maybe she liked to cook, too.

He had no idea who she was or where she'd come from, but he certainly could have done worse. What the hell. He'd always believed in making the best of a situation, hadn't he? Now all he had to do was make his arm obey his brain and reach for her…

"Mr. Blackwolf," she said softly, those beautiful eyes of hers narrowing with concern. "How are you feeling?"

Mr. Blackwolf? Somehow he doubted that she'd be so formal if he'd...if they'd...

He glanced around the room. Not his bedroom, he realized. Or anyone's bedroom for that matter. He wasn't even in a bed. He was lying on some kind of vinyl-cushioned table. In an office. A *doctor's* office.

That's when he remembered.

His fantasy shattered, he slammed his eyes shut and groaned.

"I'll get the doctor."

"No." He managed the single word through desert-dry lips. "Wait."

He opened his eyes again, watched her hesitate.

"My plane," he said hoarsely.

"Quincy towed it out of the lake." She stepped closer, frowned at him. "Let's just worry about you right now, shall we?"

"Well, since I seem to be alive and in one piece, there's not much to worry about, is there?" He rose on one elbow, winced at the movement, then swung his legs around and sat. When the room started to spin, he grabbed the edge of the table.

"Spoken like a real man." She shook her head at him and smiled. "Just be careful if you beat that chest of yours, Tarzan. With two bruised ribs, it might smart a little."

Damn. He rubbed at his chest. It did feel as if an elephant had done a tap dance on top of him. When the room finally righted itself again, he narrowed his gaze at the woman. The image of a slender hand unbuckling his seat belt flashed in his mind, the sound of someone yelling at him over the thundering storm, then the press of a feminine body against his, forcing him to walk.

Holly Douglas.

Well, fate certainly did have a strange sense of humor, he thought wryly. He'd come here to change this woman's life and she'd ended up saving his. He just might laugh if he wasn't certain it would hurt.

The ends of her hair were still damp, he noted, though her clothes were dry. She'd obviously changed. He glanced down at what he was wearing. Or should he say, what he *wasn't* wearing. The thin blue cotton hospital gown he had on barely covered his thighs. And underneath, the only thing he wore was skin. Terrific. He was not only weak as a kitten, he was practically naked. Not exactly the scenario he'd envisioned as their first meeting.

"Well, Miss Douglas, it seems that you have me at a disadvantage. If you could just bring me my—"

"How did you know my name?"

It seemed as though all her senses had gone on alert. Her eyes narrowed sharply, the smile that had played on her lips faded.

Dammit. He wasn't ready to tell her who he really was or why he was here. Especially now, under these circumstances.

"Who else would be out in a storm waiting for a shipment but the person who placed the order?" He shrugged, did his best to ignore the pain that shot through his shoulder. "Now if you don't mind, I'd really like my clothes."

Her shoulders relaxed, then she turned and moved toward a chair in the corner of the room. In spite of the throbbing ache that started at his temple and ended with his toes, Guy couldn't help but admire the snug fit of denim over the woman's behind and the long stretch of shapely legs. And to say he hadn't noticed the gentle curve of breasts under her navy turtleneck sweater would be a big lie, too. Hell, he might be hurting, but he wasn't dead.

"Your shirt had blood on it and your jeans were ripped." She picked up a brown paper shopping bag off the chair and brought it to him. "I brought some clothes from my store that ought to fit you. But you really should wait until Doc gets back before you try anything too physical."

He glanced in the bag at the new jeans and blue flannel shirt. "Thanks. I'll take my chances."

"I threw in some boxers, too."

He looked at her, saw a hint of a smile on those gorgeous lips of hers, wondered if she'd guessed he wore boxers, or had found out firsthand. Someone had obviously undressed him, and she had been the one to bring him in...

He decided he didn't want to know. What he wanted to know, was when he could get the hell out of here.

"Miss Douglas—" He started to stand, determined to get dressed with or without an audience, but the second his feet hit the gray speckled tile floor, his legs buckled. She moved quickly, had her arms around his waist before he went down.

"Holly." She sucked in a breath, held him steady. "It's kind of a rule of mine that all the men I pull from burning planes and buy underwear for call me by my first name.''

Her arms felt nice around him. Very nice. Firm, but warm and soft. But her arms weren't the only thing that felt nice. Her breasts were also pressed against his chest. And like her arms, they were also firm, but warm and soft. His bruised ribs didn't seem to mind the pressure one little bit. The faint scent of strawberries and something else...mint, he realized, drifted from her damp hair and though he knew it wasn't wise, he simply let himself enjoy the moment. Holly.

Holly knew that she should let go of the man. He seemed to be standing on his own just fine now and didn't need her assistance any longer. But she really couldn't be certain, could she? And besides, if he did fall, she'd have one hell of a time getting him up off the floor by herself. He was a good six-foot-three, at least seven or eight inches taller than she was. Built solid as a Western red cedar. So she held on, just another moment or two, she told herself, until she was sure he was all right.

He still had the scent of the storm on him, she noticed, and his skin radiated heat with the intensity of a wood furnace. It had been a long time since she'd had her arms around a man—a nearly naked man at that—and against her wishes, her body reacted to the touch of male against female with a mind of its own.

''It seems that I owe you a thank you—again,'' he said quietly.

''You're welcome.'' She heard the breathless quality in her voice, felt her cheeks warm at her foolishness. She was just feeling responsible for the man, that was all, she told herself. He'd nearly died, for heaven's sake. Emotions were running a little high.

And still she didn't move.

He didn't move, either.

She heard the thud of his heart under her ear, felt the rock-hard muscle of his chest against her cheek. His large hands were splayed over her back, and suddenly Holly wasn't certain who was holding who up.

"You all right now?"

"Fine." His breath skimmed the top of her head. "Just fine."

"Well, okay, then I suppose we should—"

The office door opened at that moment and Dr. Eaton—"Doc" to the people of Twin Pines—walked into the room. He was the only doctor in town, a youthful version of St. Nick without the beard: sparkling blue eyes under round wired spectacles, rosy cheeks, thick white hair he wore pulled back into a ponytail. The man even had a jolly laugh. When he glanced up from the file in his hands and took in the sight of Holly embracing his most recent patient, he raised one bushy eyebrow.

"Well," Doc said as he moved into the room, "looks like someone's feeling better."

Not certain if the doctor was referring to her or his patient, Holly shoved away from Guy. He gave a grunt of pain at the sudden movement, then gripped the edge of the table to steady himself.

"He insists on getting up and dressed," she explained quickly. A little *too* quickly. She shoved her hands into the back pockets of her jeans. "Maybe he'll listen to you, Doc."

"If you couldn't convince him, I can't imagine he'd listen to an old geezer like me." Doc smiled at Guy. "How's that head of yours feeling?"

"Like my bungee cord snapped." Guy scooted back up on the table.

Dr. Eaton chuckled. "You're a lucky man, Mr. Blackwolf. Very few men survive a plane crash with little more than a few stitches in their head and a couple of bruised ribs." He pulled a slender, silver flashlight out of his white coat pocket and turned it on. "'Course, tomorrow you're also going to be ten different shades of black and blue. Look at the light here, please, and follow with your eyes only."

While Dr. Eaton examined Guy, Holly stood back, hands still shoved into her back pockets. She told herself to keep her eyes on the table in the corner where Doc kept clear glass containers of cotton balls and swabs and latex gloves. But her gaze kept drifting to a pair of bare legs that dangled over the edge of the table.

How could a woman ignore such blatant masculinity? She'd seen her share of male legs before; she was hardly a blushing teenager. But Blackwolf's legs were extraordinary. Long and powerful, thighs and calves defined by well-honed muscles, a lightning bolt-shaped scar that ran upward from his right knee and disappeared under the gown he wore. And while the doctor tested the pilot's reflexes, Holly found herself wondering just how far up his thigh the scar continued and what sort of injury had caused it.

And as her gaze swept down again, she also wondered—just for a moment—what that light sprinkling of coarse, dark hair might feel like against her own smooth legs. She chided herself at such a thought, but for heaven's sake, what harm did a little wondering ever do? He had nice feet, too, she noted. Large, with straight, smooth toes and clipped nails.

"Holly?"

"What?" The single word came out as a guilty squeak. Her heart jumped, and she jerked her gaze up at the sound of her name. Both Blackwolf and Doc were staring at her. She cleared her throat. "I'm sorry. Did you say something?"

"I asked if you'd mind calling Russ over at the lodge. Mr. Blackwolf will need a room where he can rest a few days before he heads back to Seattle and both rooms here at clinic are already occupied."

"Oh, sure."

She closed the door behind her on her way to the outer office, but not before she caught a glimpse of Blackwolf shrugging out of his gown so the doctor could check his ribs. At the brief sight of the pilot's broad, muscled chest—complete with the same coarse, dark hair as she'd seen on his legs—Holly's pulse skipped.

No question about it, Holly thought as she picked up the phone and punched buttons. Guy Blackwolf was one fine specimen of a man.

She spoke to Russ at the lodge, Ned at the Hardware Store, Clay at the sheriff's office, then Quincy at the auto repair shop and Mitch Walker, who owned a small construction company just outside of Twin Pines.

No luck.

With a sigh, Holly stared at the closed examination room door.''

Like it or not, saving Guy Blackwolf had made him her responsibility.

Two

How in the world was a five-foot-eight, one-hundred-twenty-pound woman supposed to get an injured, six-foot-three, two-hundred-pound, solid-muscled man up twenty steps of stairs?

Slowly, Holly decided as she parked her car behind her store. Through the light mist of rain enveloping her windshield, she frowned at the steep redwood planks leading to her apartment.

"Here we are." She shut off her car's engine and looked at her passenger. He had a bandage over the stitches on his temple, and his right eye looked as if it had waltzed into an angry logger's fist. He looked wounded, ruggedly handsome and just a touch dangerous. "Think you can make it up those stairs?"

He glanced at the steps. "Piece of cake."

"Right." She slid out of the driver's seat, thankful

that the earlier downpour had settled into a heavy drizzle. She came around the car, frowned when she saw he'd already opened the door and stepped out before she could reach him. She sucked in a breath when his knees started to buckle, watched as he grasped the edge of the door to steady himself.

"Maybe I should go get some help," she said warily.

He shook his head. "Just give me a second. I'm fine."

He wasn't fine at all, she thought, though she had to admit he *looked* extremely fine in the clothes she'd brought him. The jeans were snug around his lean hips, the blue flannel shirt cut across his broad shoulders as if it had been tailor-made for him. She'd brought him boots, as well, but they'd been too small, so he'd had to wear the same ones he'd had on when she'd pulled him out of the plane and into the lake.

And now, with no place else for him to go, she was bringing him home.

Resigned to her fate, she slipped an arm around his waist, felt the heat of his body against hers. "You ready?"

He nodded, draped an arm around her shoulders. "You really don't have to do this, you know. There's got to be a bed or sofa somewhere in this town I can crash on for a couple of days."

"Like I told you back at Doc's office, the lodge is full of tourists in for the fishing season and the storm stranded a group of backpackers from Anchorage." She paused at the foot of the stairs, shifted her weight. "At the moment, there isn't an empty bed in town.

Here we go. Let's take it slow and easy, one step at a time.''

They made it halfway up the steps when she felt him sway slightly. She'd never be able to hold him if he went down. They'd both end up in a pile at the bottom of the stairs. She almost wished she had accepted Doc's offer to help.

"Don't you dare quit on me when the going gets tough.'' She tightened her hold and shoved him toward the next step. ''There's a warm bed and a bottle of Jack Daniel's at the top of these stairs. Now move it.''

"Words to heat a man's blood, darlin','' he muttered, but the tight set of his strong jaw and the death grip he had on her shoulders told Holly that doing the wild thing was the last thing he had on his mind.

They were both soaked by the time they reached the top of the steps. Holly yanked the door open and they stumbled into her living room, dripping water on her brown tiled entry. She maneuvered Guy to the small sofa in the center of the room and dumped him there. They were both breathing heavy.

"I'm all wet.'' He started to rise, but she pushed gently on his shoulders and eased him back.

"It's leather,'' she said. ''A little water won't hurt it. You just stay right there.''

Her apartment was small, a cozy one-bedroom with hardwood floors, knotty pine walls and a floor-to-ceiling river stone fireplace. She'd loved it the moment she'd laid eyes on it, even though the dirt and dust had been a foot thick and the current residents, a family of gray squirrels, had protested angrily at her intrusion. She'd scrubbed the place spotless, learned how to replace broken water pipes and cracked tile, seal a leaky roof, repair cabinet drawers. Over the next several months she'd slowly made it her own: an old pie safe from a local flea market she'd stenciled leaves on, a tiny oak kitchen table and two ladder-back chairs she'd stripped and restained, a pine wooden crate that had once shipped cans of salmon was now an end table for her sofa.

She was as far as she could be from the tiny, dust-dry Texas trailer park where her mother had raised her. And still, she thought, it wasn't far enough. But she felt more at home here in Twin Pines than she had anywhere else. For the first time in her life, she was happy.

She loved everything about the small, back country town. No one had to prove themselves to anyone here. No one judged or criticized or set impossible standards.

Not that the town was immune to gossip, of course. Gossip was the number one pastime in Twin Pines, and several of the residents had turned it into an art form. When the auxiliary ladies met on Wednesday afternoons at Holly's general store, the gathering was more of a theater performance than a meeting, each lady attempting to outdo the next with a current little tidbit of hearsay. Stories were embellished and acted out with dramatic enthusiasm, and though the truth might be stretched, the tales were never malicious or hurtful. And Holly knew that in spite of all the talk, there wasn't a resident in Twin Pines who wouldn't be there for their neighbor if they were needed.

Three years ago she wouldn't have believed that such a place existed. Or that she could ever be a part of it. But it *did* exist and she *was* a part of it, she thought with a smile. Twin Pines was her life now. The town, the people, her store. The kids at Twin Pines' Elementary she read stories to every Tuesday and Thursday afternoons. She wouldn't trade or give up one little part of any of that. Not for anything or anyone.

She hurried to her hall cupboard and grabbed a handful of towels, then came back into the living room and tossed one at him as she bent down and reached for his boots. "We've got to get your clothes off and get you in bed."

"So I did die." Smiling, he laid his head back and closed his eyes. "And this is heaven. Ouch!"

His eyes flew open again when she yanked his wet boot off. "Or maybe not," he said, frowning. She smiled sweetly and turned her attention to his other foot.

"Dry your hair, Blackwolf." She pulled on his second boot, but it clung stubbornly. She pulled harder and finally it came free with a sucking pop. "And take off that shirt."

"I'm kinda shy. Maybe if you took yours off first, I'd feel more comfortable."

Holly arched a brow at him as she glanced up. The glint in his pale gray eyes was mischievous, but his face was pasty-white, his voice heavy with exhaustion.

"Blackwolf..." she warned.

"Can't blame a guy for trying," he muttered and reached for the towel she'd tossed at him.

She was torn between laughing at him or scowling. She doubted he had enough strength to make it to the bed, let alone pursue any lustful fantasies. And it was just about time for the pain medication Doc had given him to kick in, as well. If she didn't get him to bed soon, he'd be out cold on her sofa.

She watched his feeble attempts to unbutton his shirt, then finally brushed his hands aside. "Let me."

"Anyone ever tell you that you're bossy?" he complained, but settled back on the sofa while her fingers quickly moved down the front of his shirt.

"All the time." Gently she tugged his shirt from the waistband of his jeans and slid the garment off, resisted the urge to press her fingers to the angry red welt that slashed across his broad chest. She held out a hand to him. "Up you go."

He took her hand, but instead of rising, he tugged her down next to him. The amusement was gone from his eyes now. "You've already gone above and beyond, Holly," he said quietly. "I'll just crash here on your couch until the morning."

"The last time you crashed, Mr. Blackwolf, I had to drag you out of a smoking plane." His hand was large, his palm callused and rough. The strength that radiated from him surprised her, as did the heat spreading up her arm into her body. She ignored that heat and concentrated instead on the task at hand, which was getting him to bed.

"You have a mild concussion and bruised ribs." She leveled a stern, schoolteacher's gaze at him. "By tomorrow you're going to have aches and pains in places you didn't know you could have aches and pains. You need a bed to sleep in, with a real mattress and lots of quiet. If you sleep out here, you'll be in my way. I'm up early for work, and I don't want to have to worry about waking you up.''

Still holding his hand, she stood. "Now are you going to get in my bed or do I have to get rough?''

"To think I used to fantasize a girl would say that to me," he said wistfully.

On a grimace he rose and once again she slipped an arm around his waist and guided him to the bedroom. He leaned against her, all hard muscle and warm skin, and in spite of herself, she felt her pulse rush at the contact.

"Sit here." She pulled the white down comforter covering her bed out of the way and helped him sit on the edge of the mattress.

He glanced from the pink floral pillows on her bed to the square mauve throw rug on the hardwood floor. A white wicker chair in the corner held an assortment of antique porcelain dolls and one overstuffed, battered-looking bear. "Nice teddy.''

Shaking her head, she moved to the window. At this time of year it never really got dark and blinds were necessary to separate day from night. "The bathroom's at the end of the hall. I'll put out a razor and toothbrush for you to use when you're ready. Towels are in the hall cupboard and—''

When she turned back to look at him, she forgot what she was going to say. Even in the semidarkness, the sight of him sitting on the edge of her bed, his chest and feet bare, his dark hair damp and rumpled, was so personal, so…intimate, she quite literally lost her breath.

"And what?"

"And…as soon as you're feeling strong enough to shower, you can help yourself to shampoo and soap," she finished, though she didn't think that was what she'd started to say. She moved to her dresser and busied herself in the top drawer, pulled out clothes she'd need later and in the morning.

"By the way," he said as he slipped under the covers. "Do I have to worry about some guy named Moose or Bear walking in here and misunderstanding why some strange man is sleeping in your bed?"

"If you're asking if I have a jealous boyfriend—" she rooted through her underwear drawer "—the answer is no."

The fact was, she'd never even had a man in her bedroom before, unless she counted Lester, the seventy-year-old carpenter who'd replaced the window opposite the bed with a gothic leaded glass window she'd found from a demolished Orthodox Russian church in Sitka. And Keegan Bodine. He'd delivered and set up the cherrywood headboard she'd bought from Auntie M's Antiques and Ammunition on Third and Main. Keegan was an outback guide in Twin Pines, thirty-two, single, good-looking. But he was just a friend. A good friend but nothing more.

Alaska was full of men like Keegan. Rugged, healthy, robust men looking for a woman. One day

Holly assumed she'd find the right one and settle down, but for now, she preferred to keep her relationships simple and she wasn't looking for love. Not the one-night kind or the permanent kind. At this moment, she loved her life just as it was: busy and full and no complications.

"What about you?" she asked, glancing over her shoulder at him. Once again, the sight of his long body stretched out in her bed made her breath catch. She quickly looked away.

"I definitely don't have a boyfriend," he said with a yawn. "Or any other entanglements, either."

She heard the heavy sound of his breathing and quietly crept toward the door. *Entanglements.* A strange, but appropriate word, she thought, and paused by the doorway to watch the steady rise and fall of his chest. Let herself wonder for just a moment what those honed muscles would feel like under her fingers, what that body would feel like—

"Hey, Holly?"

She jumped at the husky, sleep-heavy sound of his voice. Guilt warmed her cheeks.

"He warned me you were difficult." His words were slurred, barely intelligible. "He didn't warn me you were so damn sexy."

He rolled away from her then and this time she was certain he was out.

He warned me you were difficult?

Who had warned him? Doc? Or maybe Quincy had said that to Guy when he'd called over to the garage and asked about his plane. But that didn't really make sense, either, she thought, shaking her head. Maybe it was just the drugs and exhaustion talking and his comment was nothing more than gibberish.

That was probably it, she decided as she quietly closed the bedroom door behind her. Difficult, my foot. She frowned. She wasn't difficult. At least, not unreasonably.

She paused, stared at the closed bedroom door.

He didn't warn me you were so damn sexy.

Those words made her blood warm. More gibberish? she wondered. Or had he meant it?

More than likely, he said that to all the women. And no doubt, with this man, there was a long line of swooning females.

Sexy? Her?

She looked at her jeans and boots, the turtleneck she wore. He certainly hadn't been referring to her clothes. Her hair was a mess from her dive in the lake, and she wasn't wearing any makeup. So what could he possibly think was sexy about her?

She laughed at her own foolishness. The man had a head injury, for heaven's sake. He was delirious. For all he knew, she could be Olive Oyl. And what did it matter anyway? He'd be gone in a few days after he recuperated, and since he wasn't a regular with the company who normally flew in shipments, she'd probably never see him again.

Shaking her head, she pushed all thoughts of Guy Blackwolf from her mind. She'd already lost nearly an entire day's work. She was bone-tired, but she still had orders to fill and bills to pay. And if there was one thing she'd learned growing up, money sure as hell didn't fall out of the sky.

* * *

Guy dreamed of double-double hamburgers, hot, greasy French fries and rich, thick chocolate shakes with whipped cream and a big, fat cherry on top. He had the burger in one hand, the shake in the other. On a sigh, he bit into the juicy meat, but suddenly it turned to shredded cardboard in his mouth. He took a gulp of the shake, but that also had the consistency of powdery sawdust.

He woke on a hoarse cough, felt a searing pain in his chest, then blinked hard and remembered where he was. In Holly Douglas's bedroom.

In her bed.

When she found out who he really was and what he was doing here, no doubt he'd be sleeping on the street.

Rising on an elbow, he reached for the glass of water on the bedstand. For the past two days, every time he'd awakened, there'd been a full glass there. He downed the water, then sank back onto the pillows. His chest burned and his head throbbed, but for the first time in two days, his mind was beginning to clear.

He'd felt, more than actually seen her presence since he'd tumbled into her bed. A soft rustle, a quiet whisper. Once or twice, the cool touch of her fingers on his forehead. And even when she wasn't in the room, he'd known that she'd been there by the faint smell of strawberries and wild mint, mixed with a scent that belonged to her alone.

He'd slipped in and out of sleep, managed to muster up just enough strength to stumble back and forth to the bathroom on his own, but that was it. He'd given his body the rest that it had needed. But now, ready or not, he was getting out of bed.

And, as the saying went, he was hungry enough to eat a bear.

Since he probably smelled like a bear, though, he thought it best to tackle a shower before food. He swung his legs over the edge of the bed, then dropped his bare feet onto the cool hardwood floor. When the room stopped moving, he rose, tugged on his jeans, grabbed the blue flannel shirt she'd given him to wear and made his way to the bathroom.

Her blue-tiled shower was small, the nozzle too low for a man his height, but the water was hot and the pressure strong. The familiar scent of strawberries filled the bathroom—her shampoo, he realized, and couldn't help himself from taking a whiff of the bottle sitting on the shower shelf. As much as he enjoyed the smell, he appreciated the unscented shampoo and fresh bar of green deodorant soap she'd left out for him on the sink countertop. A guy couldn't very well go around smelling like strawberries, after all.

He brushed his teeth, shaved, and except for the fact that every bone in his body ached, he nearly felt human again. Now the most pressing problem was the empty pit in his stomach.

On his way to the kitchen, though, he spotted the phone on the table beside her sofa. He needed to call Flynn and give the man an update on the situation here, but hadn't had an opportunity since he'd dumped his plane into the lake. With Holly gone, there was no better time than now.

Guy glanced around the quiet apartment. His brain

had been muddled when she'd brought him in here that first day, and he hadn't gotten a good look at the place. The furnishings were simple, but comfortable, a blend of woodsy and feminine, old and new. There were several books on a shelf beside the fireplace. Mysteries, biographies and romance, plus a new Jonathan Kellerman he'd bought himself last week but hadn't had time to read. There were also several children's books, which he found curious. From what Flynn had told him, she'd never been married. Of course, that certainly didn't preclude her from having a child, but it was obvious that none lived here.

He picked up the phone, used his calling card to dial the Texas number, then sat down on the sofa, ignoring the pain that shot through his right leg when he bent his knee.

A deep, familiar voice answered on the third ring.

"Hey, Dog-Man." From the day Flynn Sinclair had brought Guy's older sister, Susan, a black labrador, Guy had used the nickname. "What's up?"

"Dammit, B.W., where the hell have you been?" Flynn growled, using his own nickname for Guy. "You were supposed to call me when you got to Twin Pines."

"Small problem." Guy glanced at a stack of opened mail on the table beside the sofa, let his gaze linger longer than anyone would consider polite. A late notice from an insurance company and a bill from a credit card company with overdue fees lay on top. "I've been laid up in bed for a couple of days."

"Yeah?" Flynn snorted. "Knowing you, there's a female involved. So what's her name?"

"Holly Douglas."

There was a pause, then a blast. "What! Dammit, B.W., I sent you there to bring the woman back to Texas to meet her family, not jump into her bed."

Guy settled back, decided to let Flynn stew for a bit. "I'm only human, pal. Before I could even think to say no, she had me out of my clothes and between the sheets."

While Flynn went on to rant at him, Guy sort of peeked at the rest of Holly's mail. An unopened letter with Ryan Fortune's return address in one corner and another bill from the electric company, also late.

After a couple of minutes, the other end of the line went quiet. "You're pulling my leg, aren't you?" Flynn said with a heavy sigh. "And I fell for it."

"Hook, line and sinker." Guy grinned, noticed a small, fat pillow on the sofa that said Home Sweet Home. "But I'm actually the one who fell. Out of the sky, into Twin Pines Lake. Miss Douglas graciously pulled me out of my plane before I became fish bait."

He went on to give details as best he could, including the twist of fate that now had him sleeping in the bed of the woman who had brought him here. And though Flynn argued, Guy told him that he wasn't leaving Twin Pines until Holly Douglas agreed to come back to Texas with him.

"You better tell her the truth soon," Flynn said. "As it is, she might ship you back here in little pieces with a bow on top, just to emphasize the point that she wants nothing to do with the Fortune family."

"I'll tell her. I just think it's something I should ease into, rather than jump with both feet." Guy heard footsteps coming up the stairs. "Gotta, go, pal."

He had the phone back on the hook and just managed to make it to the kitchen when she walked in the front door. She'd done something different with her thick chestnut hair, he noted, casually piled it on top of her head and secured it with a large tortoiseshell clip. She wore a light blue denim jacket over a snug white top, jeans that hugged her slender hips and black suede lace-up hiking boots.

There wasn't one item of clothing that by itself would remotely be considered sexy, and still he felt his pulse jump. He couldn't help but wonder what he might find under all that smooth denim and cotton. More cotton? Lace?

Silk, he decided, watching her close the door behind her. Something in the way she moved. Smooth as silk.

She caught sight of him in the kitchen and hesitated, then narrowed those golden lady-tiger eyes at him.

"You better talk fast, Blackwolf," she said tightly and advanced on him.

Guy's gaze dropped to the black leather sports bag she held in her left hand. *His* bag. He hadn't needed it before, but she'd obviously retrieved it from the plane. He struggled to remember what he kept packed in there. A couple of T-shirts, fresh pair of jeans, some toiletries. A paperback, but he couldn't recall which one. Nothing he could think of that would give him away.

She set the bag on the kitchen table and folded her arms. "You've got some explaining to do, mister, and it better be good."

Three

"I should toss you out of here on your butt right now." Holly pressed her lips into a stern line. "What have you got to say for yourself?"

"Uh…" He stared at his sports bag on the table, then remembered the letter he'd shoved in there before he'd left. It was from Flynn, on Fortune stationery. Guy knew that if Holly had seen it, he was a dead man. He hesitated, then looked back at her. "I'm sorry?"

She gave an unladylike snort. "Typical male response, spoken with typical lack of sincerity. I want to know what you were thinking?"

He paused, then said carefully, "I wasn't?"

"You got that right." Pulling a kitchen chair from the table, she thrust a finger at it. "Sit."

"Yes, ma'am." He sat.

"And don't use that tone with me, either."

"No, ma'am."

"You got up and took a shower by yourself."

So that's what she was upset about, he thought with a mixture of relief and surprise. It wasn't really anger he saw in her narrowed gaze. It was concern.

When was the last time a woman had fussed over him? he wondered. His mother had run off when he was eleven. Other than his sister, no one had really worried about him since he was a kid. And even she was gone now.

But this was hardly the time to think about Susan. Those thoughts he saved for late at night, when he was alone with a bottle of whiskey and the few photographs of his sister that he kept in the bottom drawer of his dresser.

He turned his attention back to Holly, felt a strange ripple of pleasure that the distress in her eyes was genuine. "Well, shoot, Miss Douglas." He reached for her hand. "I would have waited for you if I'd known you wanted to join me. But I'm sure I missed a spot or two. I wouldn't mind taking another one if it would make you happy."

"The only dirty spot you missed was your mind." She yanked her hand away. "For two days you've barely had the strength to get out of bed and make it ten feet to the bathroom. What would I have done if you'd passed out in the shower?"

"Holly, I'm fine." He took her hand again, even though she resisted. "I appreciate your concern, but really, I'm okay. I'm not going to pass out."

"See that you don't," she said firmly, but her

words lacked heat. "I promised Doc I'd make sure you didn't crack that head of yours open again."

Her fingers were long and slender, her skin warm and smooth against his palm. "The last thing we want to do is upset Doc."

"Absolutely," she murmured. Her gaze dropped to their linked hands. "That's the last thing we'd want to do."

"Holly," he said her name softly, tugged her down to sit on the chair beside him. "I do appreciate all you've done for me. Fishing me out of the lake and taking me to the doctor, bringing me home. Letting me sleep in your bed. For all you know, I'm a serial killer or an escapee from a mental ward."

"How do you know you aren't the one taking the chance?" she said, and he saw the smile in her eyes as she lifted her gaze to his. "Did you see the movie, *Misery?* For all *you* know, my back garden is filled with the bones of all the men I've brought home. The calcium is wonderful for roses, you know."

"Your hands don't feel like you've been digging in dirt." He traced the ridge of her knuckles with his thumb. "They're much too soft and delicate."

She swayed slightly toward him. "Things aren't always what they seem."

He hesitated at her words, felt the first prick of guilt that he hadn't been completely honest with her yet. But he hadn't lied to her exactly, either. He'd simply withheld information.

"Holly," he said softly. "I want you to know that you can trust me."

She arched a brow at him, tilted her head. "Trust

is something that has to be earned, Guy. I don't know you that well."

"Sure you do," he said evenly. "Maybe not what kind of music I like or my favorite sport or even what model car I drive. But you know me, probably better than most people."

It was the oddest thing for him to say, Holly thought, and yet she did feel as if she knew him. She didn't know why she felt that way, but from the moment she'd dragged him out of that plane, there'd been something between them she couldn't explain. Some strange connection. Two days of watching over him, worrying that he was all right had only intensified that connection.

But trust him? She'd learned at a young age how blind trust could destroy lives and break hearts. Trust was precious to her, sacred, and she wasn't ready to give it to this man so quickly or so easily.

The texture of his hand was rough against her own, his skin deeply tanned. His wet, black hair was slicked back from his freshly shaved face, a face shaped from rugged angles and sharp lines, a nose bent across the bridge, brows dark and foreboding, a sensuous mouth and square jaw. Intense pale gray eyes, wolf eyes, that made her breath catch every time she looked into them. He smelled like soap and shampoo and man.

She wasn't certain exactly how or when the air in her kitchen had grown so thick, or why she was having such difficulty remembering the reason she'd come up here in the first place—especially since she had so much work to do downstairs in her general store. And she wasn't certain at all why she was standing here, letting this man hold her hand and draw her close as if they were lovers instead of just simple acquaintances.

She watched Guy's thumb draw lazy circles over her knuckles, felt the heat curl up her arm, and knew there was nothing simple at all between them. It was as complex as it was dark and erotic. Seductive.

Confusing.

She didn't want this. These feelings, this complication. There was chemistry between them, she'd be lying to herself if she denied that. It was stronger than anything she'd ever experienced before. But Guy Blackwolf was just passing through. It was fine to flirt a little, but that was all. At a very basic level, she knew that anything more would be very risky. And while she might take risks with her business, her money or even her life, she did not take risks with her heart. The price was too great.

"So." She pulled her hand away and stood, was annoyed with the fact that her knees were weak. "You ready for some food?"

He grinned at her. "I thought you'd never ask."

"I have to warn you, though—" she opened the pantry beside her refrigerator and busied herself by moving the six cans in there from one side to the other "—I don't cook. Chicken Noodle or Beef with Stars?"

"You don't cook? And here I thought I'd found the perfect woman." He sighed mournfully. "Ah, well. Beef with Stars is fine."

Rolling her eyes, she pulled a saucepan from a bottom cupboard, then reached for a can opener in the drawer. "Quincy brought over your bag from your plane. Now that you're on your feet, I'm sure there are some things in there you can use."

"Thanks."

"He parked your plane in the lot behind his shop," she said and hooked the opener onto the can. "In a day or two, when you're steady on your feet, I can take you over so you can assess the damage. Quincy said the tail section was hit pretty bad, but you can—"

At the touch of his hand on her arm, the opener slipped off the can. She'd been so busy rambling on, she hadn't even heard him come up behind her.

"I can manage from here." He took the opener from her. "I'm sure you've got a lot of other things to do besides taking care of me."

She did, but with him standing so close in her small kitchen, she couldn't think of what even one of those things were. She watched him open the can and dump the soup into the pan she'd set on the stove, then turn on the flame underneath.

"Bowls are in the cupboard to your right," she said. "Silverware in the drawer to your left. There might even be some cookies in the pantry."

"Okay."

"Well, I've got to get back to work." She started to back away and stumbled over a chair. He reached out a hand to steady her and once again it was difficult to think clearly.

"Ah, television reception is decent, but I only get a couple of channels. If your head starts to bother you, there's aspirin in the bathroom cabinet, or if you need a—''

"Holly, I'm fine. Go."

"Right." She headed for the door, paused. "Oh, I think there are cookies in the pantry, too."

He smiled. "You mentioned that. Thanks."

Darn it. She'd been around plenty of handsome, virile men and they never made her blush or stumble over her own feet or repeat herself. Guy Blackwolf was really starting to annoy her.

"Holly?"

Her hand was on the knob when she glanced over her shoulder and saw him watching her with those wolf eyes of his.

"I think you should sleep in the bedroom tonight."

Her pulse quickened as she stared at him. Had she been so transparent in her attraction to him that he assumed she would just jump into bed with him? Narrowing her gaze, she said coolly, "Look, Blackwolf, just because you're sort of a good-looking guy with a decent enough body doesn't mean that every woman is just waiting around for an invitation to sleep with you. Thanks, but no thanks."

His brow rose. "I was just offering to take the sofa tonight," he said with a grin. "But thanks anyway for the sort-of-almost compliment. I think."

"Oh. Sorry." Darn it, darn it. She'd done it again. Made a complete fool out of herself. "I just thought that you—I mean, I assumed that… Oh, never mind."

Quickly, before he could see the blush that was working its way up her neck, she hurried out the door, not quite certain if she was relieved or disappointed.

* * *

"What do you mean, you're leaving! You can't leave me, not now. Do I mean nothing to you?"

"You're everything to me. That's why I must leave. Don't you see?"

A bag of chocolate chip cookies in one hand, the remote in his other, Guy sat on the sofa and watched the only channel where he'd been able to find a semi-clear reception. After Holly had left earlier, he'd had a dizzy spell and been forced to lay low for a while. He'd tried to read, but the words had blurred, so he'd been left with the company of the TV.

From what he'd been able to figure out so far, the soap opera, *Storm's Cove,* took place in a small Seattle seaside community that was spilling over with sex and scandal. Guy had lived in Seattle for five years and was amazed that such lust and treachery existed right under his nose.

At the moment, a blonde named Victoria had caught Gerald, the man she loved, packing a bag and getting ready to run out on her.

"I see nothing," Victoria wailed. "Only that you're throwing our love away, as if I was nothing more to you than an old shoe."

"How can you say that?" Gerald cried. "You would never be an old shoe to me, Cynthia. Never. You know I love you."

"Lies! Lies! Everything's been a lie. You came back from the dead to me and to Emily, the daughter you never knew you had, only to leave us again. How can I live if you go?"

Gerald grabbed the blonde's shoulders, his movie

star face a mask of anguish. "Don't say that, Victoria. Don't ever say that. I'll come back to you and Emily, I promise, but not until I find the person responsible for my brother's death."

How could anyone watch this cornball stuff? he wondered as he took a healthy bite of another cookie. Jeez, get real. Who cared if the jerk left or not? And—

Suddenly the room Gerald and Victoria had been standing in exploded, then burst into flames. *Now* we're talking, Guy thought, settling back on the sofa. The scene cut away to a toilet bowl cleaner commercial. He shoved in two more cookies while waiting for the show to return, but only music and credits came back. He stared openmouthed at the TV. That's how they were going to leave it? Just like that? With not even a hint of what happened to poor Victoria and Gerald?

He figured that sort of cheap tactic brought the viewers back day after day, but he'd be damned if he'd let himself be manipulated that easily. It was just a TV show, for crying out loud. With actors reading their lines.

Scowling, he turned the television off and wandered into the kitchen to put the cookies away.

It was a cozy kitchen, he thought. Small, but tidy, with oak-stained cabinets and blue checked curtains on the window over the sink. Yellow ceramic canisters were lined up neatly on the white Formica countertop and a black-and-white hand-painted cutout of a cow hung on the wall beside the stove. He touched the miniature copper bell on the cow's neck, and it tinkled softly.

Flynn hadn't told him much about Holly, Guy realized. He knew she was from Dallas, that she'd been raised only a hundred miles from where Guy's family had lived. Like spitting to the corner, so the saying went. Yet here she was in Twin Pines, running her own business, working long hours. Saving pilots who crashed their planes in the lake, then taking them home to recuperate in her bed. Same old things that every other woman did on a daily basis.

He'd never met a woman like her. Maybe he'd met some that were as beautiful, some that had a terrific body like hers, some that made him laugh like she did.

But he'd never met a woman who was all those things, or one that constantly crept into his mind. One that made his pulse race with a look, his blood heat with a simple touch.

He'd wanted to kiss her earlier. It surprised him just how much. Almost as much as it surprised him that he hadn't. Sex was comfortable to him. If a man and woman were attracted to each other, then the rest was easy. He was certain that Holly was attracted to him, he'd seen it in the rush of emotions in her face when he'd held her hand, when he'd stood beside her at the stove.

When he'd said she should sleep in the bed tonight.

Remembering the surprise, then the indignation on her face, he couldn't help but smile. She'd thought he meant sleep with him. The gaze she'd leveled at him could have formed icicles on molten lava. And still, even in her obvious irritation with him, there was also a response: the catch in her breath, the sparks of gold in her eyes, the soft flush on her cheeks. He recognized desire, had felt more than a tug of it himself toward the woman. Okay, a *lot* more than a tug, he conceded.

Under normal circumstances, he would play the game, enjoy it. But this was different. He'd come here as a favor to a friend, to talk to Holly, not seduce her or sleep with her.

And there was still that little issue of confessing why he was here, too. He had a strong feeling that she was going to feed him to the bears when she found out he hadn't been completely honest with her. He knew he needed to tell her, but he just needed another day or two. He had nowhere else to go and until his plane was repaired, if it *could* be repaired, he was stuck here.

And if he had to be stuck somewhere, this wasn't such a bad place, he thought with a smile. He glanced around the comfortable apartment, thought about Holly coming home, the two of them spending the evening together. So maybe he couldn't kiss her or seduce her, but that didn't mean he couldn't enjoy the company of a beautiful, desirable woman. Nothing wrong with that. And if they shared a little wine and conversation, there was nothing wrong with that, either.

He glanced at the clock on the stove. It was nearly six-thirty. He'd heard her mention that she closed the store at six, so she should be home any time now. Maybe she'd fuss over him some more, the way she had this afternoon. If she really wanted to, then he supposed he could tolerate it. Why not let her just—

The front door flew open and Holly rushed in. He watched as she hurried toward him, a white paper sack in her hands.

"I'm late," she gasped, thrusting the bag at him.

"For a very important date?" he teased.

"Yes." She spun and flew toward her bedroom.

Yes?

He stared at the bedroom door and barely had time to blink before she zipped across the hall into the bathroom. He heard the shower come on, but didn't even have time to conjure up any wicked fantasies before it was off again. He heard her muttering, then the slam of the medicine cabinet.

She really *did* have a date? As in, going out with a man?

He furrowed his brow. Maybe it wasn't a *date* date. Maybe it was a town meeting, or maybe she was going out with a girlfriend. Or she could be—

The knock at the front door made his brow furrow deeper. When he opened the door, he was eye-to-eye with a dark-haired man who had arms the size of oak tree trunks. He wore a white shirt, dress jeans and black cowboy boots. He'd hooked a black Western-style black sport coat on one finger and slung it over his shoulder.

Guy disliked him on sight.

"You must be Guy Blackwolf." The man's smile was friendly, as was the hand he extended. "Keegan Bodine."

"Keegan." Guy nodded, knew that he was acting stupid when he gripped the offered hand with more force than necessary, but couldn't help feeling smug when the other man let loose first.

"Holly told me about you," Keegan said cheerfully. "How's the head?"

"Fine. Just fine," he lied. His head was pounding like a Kodo drummer. "Ah, why don't you come on in? I think Holly will be out in just a minute."

At the sound of a crash from the bathroom, followed by a muffled curse, both men turned their heads.

"Well, maybe two minutes," Guy corrected.

"No sweat."

Keegan moved to the sofa and sank down on the cushions, rested his arm comfortably on the back of the couch. Guy was reminded of a German shepherd he had once had who would curl up on a foot rug at the back door. That was his spot and he knew it. Keegan had that look, Guy thought.

"I know most of the regular pilots that bring in air deliveries to Twin Pines," Keegan said. "I've never seen you before. How long have you been with Pelican?"

A simple question, asked casually. But behind the man's laid-back demeanor and easy smile, Guy recognized the suspicion, the mistrust. Hell, he'd feel the same way if the situation was reversed. What he couldn't read was exactly what Keegan and Holly's relationship was. Lovers? He didn't think so. Friends? Yes, but maybe more?

Whatever it was, Guy certainly intended to find out.

"Actually, I don't work for Pelican," Guy said carefully. "Sometimes I trade jobs with one of the guys there. When I heard you've got trout the size of ponies in that lake of yours, I thought I might take a few days and do some fishing.''

''We've got some decent rainbow.'' Keegan stretched out one long leg and grinned. ''And an occasional pilot who drops out of the sky.''

To anyone listening, the conversation would just sound like social chitchat. But Guy knew better. The real question was: *So who the hell are you and what the hell are you doing in Holly's apartment?*

''I could use a good pilot with a seaplane to make runs for my company. Mostly to the larger lakes in the inner regions that are hard to reach,'' Keegan said. ''You interested?''

Guy knew perfectly well that Keegan wasn't offering work. What the other man wanted to know was, ''When are you leaving and have you got any plans on coming back?'' And though he wasn't interested, Guy couldn't resist ruffling the other man's feathers. ''Maybe. What's your company?''

''Outback Excursions. Mostly tourist stuff, an occasional nature photographer or wildlife research program group.''

''I'll let you—''

''Sorry I took so long.''

Guy turned at the sound of Holly's voice. And forgot to breathe.

She wore a sleeveless dress the color of lilacs. Long and flowing, scooped at the neck, with front buttons that ended just above her knee. When she moved, the fabric parted just enough to show the curve of her slender calves. Her sandals were white and strappy, her toes painted pretty pink. He'd thought she was sexy in her jeans and boots and casual T-shirts. But dressed like this, soft and feminine, with her hair flowing around her smooth shoulders and her lips brushed rosy pink, it was enough to bring a man to his knees.

Keegan seemed surprised, as well. He'd risen from the sofa and the look of utter male approval on his face annoyed the hell out of Guy. He knew it shouldn't. What right did he have to feelings of…what? Jealousy? He ground his teeth at the word. He wasn't a jealous kind of guy. At least, he never had been. But with Holly it felt different. He felt protective. And maybe a little possessive, too. After all, she'd saved his life. That was certainly a reason to feel a connection with her, a bond.

That and the fact that he'd come here to help her, to unite her with her family. And not just any family, but the Fortunes. One of the wealthiest, most powerful families in Texas. There were some people who might take advantage of her if they knew that one day she might inherit some of that money.

"Thanks, Guy, for keeping Keegan company." Holly reached for her purse on the table beside the sofa. "I'm glad you two got a chance to talk."

"My pleasure." Guy glanced at Keegan, who met his steady gaze. There was still indecision in the other man's eyes, doubt, and in spite of himself, Guy couldn't help but feel pleased.

"The pleasure's all mine," Keegan said with a grin, and Guy knew Keegan wasn't referring to their conversation, but to Holly.

Was she his? Guy wondered, still not certain, irritated that it mattered so much to him.

"I'll try not to wake you if I'm late." Holly opened a small coat closet just inside the front door. She pulled on a little white sweater and slipped it on. "If you need anything, just help yourself to whatever you'd like."

"Thanks." He looked at Keegan and smiled. "I'll do that."

Keegan arched a brow, then placed a hand on Holly's back. "You ready?"

After they left, Guy stared at the closed door. So much for a quiet evening with a beautiful woman, he thought with a frown.

He glanced at the bag that Holly had given him when she'd come home, realized he'd been holding it the entire time. Inside was a double-double hamburger and fries.

Except for the chocolate shake, exactly what he'd been dreaming about earlier in the day.

Help yourself to whatever you like.

He looked back at the door, thought about the curves her lilac dress had displayed, wondered what those curves would feel like underneath him without that dress. Wondered what she would taste like...

And since he couldn't help himself to what he really wanted, he went into the kitchen to eat his dinner alone.

Four

Holly smelled pizza when she opened the door to her apartment just before midnight. She paused, breathed the fragrant scent deep into her lungs. Pepperoni, if her nose served her right. Like a moth to the flame, she followed the delicious aroma into the kitchen. The box sat on the table in front of Guy, who currently had a hot game of solitaire going on. He had an unlit cigar clamped in the corner of his mouth and a baseball cap turned backward on his head.

"Cinderella returns with mere minutes to spare." He glanced up at her, counted out three more cards and flipped them over. "Where's Prince Charmin—I mean Charming? Still at the ball?"

"It was a birthday party for Alexis, his younger sister, if you must know." She tossed her purse on the table and sat down. "He would have come in and said hello, but he's leading a three-day survival excursion into Devil's Canyon in the morning for a group of six. He sends his regards. Said he'd take you out on the lake when he got back.''

"Fishing?" He took the cigar out of his mouth and looked at her skeptically.

"Something like that." What Keegan had *actually* said was that he'd like to use Guy for bait. But she didn't think it was a good idea to mention that. She'd sensed enough tension between the two men as it was. She nodded at the cards in front of him. "Who's winning?"

He looked insulted she'd even asked. "Five-two, my lead."

She arched a brow. "Impressive."

"So the women tell me." He wiggled his eyebrows. "You should see me play the Captain Blaster video game. I would dazzle you."

"Blackwolf, I'm beginning to understand why you're a pilot. You're so full of hot air, your feet won't stay on the ground." She slipped off her sandals and leaned back in her chair. "So tell me. Why are you a pilot?"

He shrugged, laid the six of spades on the seven of hearts. "I grew up behind a small airstrip. I'd watch those two-seater planes take off, and I'd wonder where they were going. How high, how far. I wanted to know what it felt like to lift up off the ground and be up in the clouds, to be in control of a machine that defied the laws of nature. I used to pedal my bike over after school and weekends and hang

around, pester the pilots with questions about planes
and flying.''

"And they took you under their wing?" she teased.

He smiled, moved a pile of cards on top of the jack
of diamonds. "Only after they found out that they
couldn't get rid of me. I had my first lesson at eigh-
teen and my license at twenty. And the rest, as they
say, is navigational history. Ta-dah—" he moved
three cards and completed every pile, then looked up
at her and grinned "—I win again. Are you dazzled
yet?"

She was, but not because he'd won a game of solitaire. It was the expression on his face, the passion
in his voice, the intensity in his eyes when he'd spoken of flying. Few people truly found a job they
loved, or their niche in life.

"How 'bout you?" he asked as he scooped up the
cards. "What are you doing up here running a general
store in the middle of nowhere?"

"Why wouldn't I be here? Just because we don't
have multiplex theaters or coffee houses on every corner doesn't make us 'nowhere,'" she defended. "In
Twin Pines, it's not important who drives the most
expensive car or who has the biggest diamond on her
finger. What's important here is people. We're a community, a lifestyle."

"A family?"

There was something in his voice, in his eyes, the
way he was watching her, waiting for her to answer,
that made her hesitate, wary even. "Yes," she said
evenly. "A family."

But family wasn't something she ever talked about,

wasn't even something she thought about. As far as she was concerned, the people of Twin Pines were the only family she had left. Certainly the only family she cared about.

"I see you had pizza delivered," she said, shifting the conversation. She lifted the pizza box lid and looked inside, nearly groaned with pleasure. Pepperoni and bell pepper. She *loved* pepperoni and bell pepper.

"'The best pizza in town.'" He pointed to the quote on the box. "'Course, I believe it's the only pizza in town, but it's pretty good. Have some."

"I already ate." Which didn't seem to make a difference to her stomach. She stared at the pizza longingly. "And besides, it's midnight."

"The best time to eat pizza."

And the best time to do other things, came the unbidden thought. She shook her head, not certain what she was saying no to.

He pushed the box closer to her. "Come on, Holly, live dangerously."

Her pulse skipped at his innocent words. Or were they innocent? she wondered. Was she imagining his eyes had narrowed and his voice had turned husky? She met his gaze, felt the intensity of his smoky-gray eyes watching her. *He* was dangerous, she thought, this man who had quite literally fallen out of the sky and into her life. He made her feel things she didn't want to feel. Not now. Not with him.

He picked up a slice of pizza, tortured her by waving it under her nose. "One little taste," he taunted.

A kaleidoscope of sensations swirled through her.

The spicy scent of herbs and of man, the deep, throaty sound of his voice, the coarse stubble of dark beard and wicked cut on his temple. Even the silly baseball cap he wore backward added a dash of charm to the image of pure male.

Her mouth watered, but not just for pizza.

"Well," she murmured, felt her defenses crumbling, "maybe just one."

Parting her lips, she delicately sank her teeth into the point of the still warm wedge of cheese and dough. It seemed as though all her senses were heightened, and she nearly moaned at the exquisite explosion of taste in her mouth.

"Shoot, that was just a nibble," he said softly. "You can do better than that."

She felt his gaze on her, saw his eyes turn the color of storm clouds as he watched her. His jaw tightened; he swallowed when she did. In her entire life, she'd never experienced anything so erotic.

She took another small bite, licked the sauce from her lips. She heard his intake of breath.

"Tell me about Keegan," he whispered.

"Keegan?" Confused, she simply stared at him. He'd leaned closer to her and she could feel the heat of his body.

"Other than the fact that he doesn't like my staying here, who is he to you?"

"We're friends," she said, then realized that she'd opened a door that was better left closed.

He arched one dark brow. "Just friends?"

"Yes, just friends." Her fingers brushed his when she took the pizza from him and the contact shimmered up her arm. She took another tiny bite, though this time she hardly tasted it. "Don't you think a man and woman can be friends?"

"Sure I do. We're friends."

Were they? she wondered as his gaze fell to her mouth, but not before she saw something in his eyes, a sadness, she thought. When he looked up again, whatever the emotion had been was gone. In its place was something she clearly recognized, something that had nothing to do with friendship.

Desire.

It was difficult to concentrate with him so close, difficult to breathe. They were moving into new territory here, moving beyond the boundaries of casual banter and mild flirting. They both knew it. The air was heavy with anticipation. With expectation.

With apprehension.

She'd always been comfortable around men before, reasonably confident and secure. But not this man. This man made her nervous and jumpy and more than a little afraid. Without thinking, she held out the pizza toward him.

"Bite?" she offered, then inwardly groaned at the slow smile that spread over his mouth.

His hand covered hers as he took a bite. He chewed slowly, watching her, then slipped the pizza from her fingers and set it down. "That really is good pizza," he said and his gaze dropped to her mouth again.

"The best," she breathed. *This is crazy.*

"Holly."

"Yes?"

"I'm going to kiss you."

No. "Okay."

Breath held, heart pounding against her ribs, she waited.

He touched her chin, then lightly traced her bottom lip with his callused thumb. A current of pleasure shimmered from that point all the way down to her bare toes.

She parted her lips, still waiting.

It was the barest whisper of his mouth against hers, a tease more than a kiss. It made every nerve ending in her body go on full alert, anxiously waiting, wanting him to deepen the contact.

He didn't. He moved to the corner of her mouth, softly nibbled, took his sweet time. Oh, and it was so sweet, she thought. So incredibly sweet.

Heat rushed through her body; her skin tingled; her breasts ached. Damn him. He hadn't even properly kissed her yet, and she was more aroused than she could ever remember. She tightened her hands into fists so she wouldn't grab him and drag him closer the way she wanted to.

When he turned his head slightly, she felt the stubble of his beard against her mouth, then her cheek. Pleasure rippled through her with an intensity that frightened her, yet somehow that only heightened her arousal, made her want more. And just when she thought she might have to hurt him if he didn't deepen the kiss, he did.

His hand cupped the back of her head, brought her closer while he slid his tongue over hers. He tasted like spices and something else, something she couldn't label. Something darker and richer and incredibly primitive. The hands she'd fisted in her lap opened and slid up his chest. She felt the heavy thud of his heart under her palms.

This wasn't possible, she thought in a haze. A simple kiss couldn't do this, couldn't turn a person inside out and upside down. Make them raw with need. It just didn't happen.

Her fingers curled into the soft cotton of his shirt. But it *was* happening, as insane as it was, and it was real. His mouth was firm and hot against hers, urgent now, demanding as he deepened the kiss the way she'd willed him to. And she was kissing him back with the same urgency, the same need. She slid her arms around his neck, wanted to crawl in his lap, wrap her arms and legs around him and lose herself completely.

His lips, the mouth she so desperately wanted on her neck and her breasts and every other place she ached, suddenly moved away.

"Holly."

Her name was a ragged whisper. She opened her eyes, blinked.

"Holly." He sucked in a breath. "We can't do this."

"We can't?"

He shook his head.

A sudden thought gripped her. Horrified at the possibility, she snatched her hands away from him. "Oh, God. Please don't tell me you're married."

"No, no. Of course I'm not married." He yanked off his baseball cap and dragged a hand through his thick, dark hair. "It's just that, we, I mean, that I—"

"Guy, it's all right. I understand." What an idiot she was, she should have realized. "I'm sorry. I wasn't thinking. You just had an accident and I'm sure you aren't quite—" she paused, knowing how sensitive men could be about that sort of thing "—up to par yet."

He stared at her as if she'd turned purple. "Holly, it's not that." He looked heavenward, then sighed heavily. "Believe me, I'm definitely up to *par.*"

"So what is it, then?" In spite of the awkwardness of the moment, she couldn't help the irritation that had crept into her voice. She'd just had the most incredible experience of her life and here he was, looking as if he was ready to run for the hills.

"I—" He faltered. "I don't want to hurt you."

Now it was her turn to stare at him. He actually assumed that one kiss between them had the power to hurt her? The man's ego was nearly as big as the foot he'd put in his mouth.

"Blackwolf," she said carefully, "if you think one little kiss can hurt me, you seriously underestimate me and ridiculously overestimate yourself."

He pressed his lips into a tight line. "That was no 'little kiss,' Holly. We both know that. All I'm saying, is that it would be a bad idea right now to take it any further."

"Well, *that* we certainly agree on." She stood slowly, eyes narrowed. "Now I know why you're so good at solitaire. With your social charms, I imagine you spend most nights alone."

"Dammit, Holly, will you just—"

"There's a pillow in the hall cupboard and a blanket in the trunk beside the sofa. I'm going to bed now.''

"Holly—''

''Good night.''

With that, she turned, silently wished him to hell, then walked away from him on legs that were still weak from his kiss.

''I was a fool. A complete fool. Please say you'll forgive me, darling.''

What a wuss, Guy thought, watching in disgust as Gerald pleaded with Victoria, who was still in the hospital following the blast that had taken out half a city block, but left her and Gerald alive. Gerald was wearing a patch over one eye, and the doctors were uncertain he'd ever be able to see from that eye again.

''It's too late.'' Victoria turned her carefully made-up face away from Gerald. And though she was lying in a hospital bed, her blond hair looked as if she'd just stepped out of a salon. "I can't be married to a man I can never trust. I'm calling off our engagement and going back to Matthew. I don't ever want to see you again.''

Guy snorted. For crying out loud. Why didn't the woman just tell him the real reason she was dumping him—because the doctors had told her that she wouldn't be able to have children due to her injuries from the explosion? Gerald would understand. Couldn't she see the guy was making an effort here? Jeez, Victoria was one coldhearted female.

The show's theme music came on as the credits

rolled. Women. Guy shook his head as he turned off the TV. Who would ever understand them?

Lord, knew, *he* certainly never would. It had been two days since he'd kissed Holly, and she'd barely said more than a dozen words to him since. He could sympathize with poor Gerald there. They'd both fumbled the ball when it came to the opposite sex, but he'd be damned if he'd beg Holly to forgive him because he'd ended a kiss that had no place to go but bed.

He knew it, and he knew that she knew it. She could call it a "simple kiss" all she wanted, but what had happened between them was as far from simple as it got.

He'd told himself—and her—that he'd put a stop to the kiss because he hadn't wanted to hurt her, that at least until she knew why he'd really come here, he needed to keep his distance.

But the truth was that when he'd kissed her, he hadn't even remotely been thinking about why he'd come here. He hadn't been thinking about Flynn, or the Fortunes or *anything* other than Holly. His only thought had been of her, of how sweet she tasted, how soft her skin was, how desperately he wanted to feel her naked against him, underneath him. How much he'd wanted to drive his body into hers and ease the ache she'd stirred inside him.

He'd nearly lost control with her. Ten seconds more and he would have. The realization of that had startled him as much as it scared him.

And *that* was the real reason he'd pulled away.

Beyond sex, there was no direction for their relationship to go. Before it got any more complicated between them, it would be best to keep things the way they were, which was nowhere. He'd contacted his insurance company, and they were sending out an adjuster next week. Once the paperwork was handled and a decision made, his plane would either be repaired or replaced. Either way, he'd be back to business as usual and out of Twin Pines. Holly didn't fit into that equation any more than he fit into hers.

As soon as she stopped being mad at him, he would talk her into going to Texas to meet her family, then he'd head back to Seattle. And that, would be that.

But first, he had to get her talking to him.

Not an easy task. She'd been slippery as a fish these past two days and had managed to somehow evade him. Sneaking in and out when he was in the bathroom or sleeping. Which meant that he'd just have to go find her. The dizzy spells were long gone and his head had cleared. He'd been cooped up in this apartment long enough.

It was time to break out.

Five

The summer afternoon was slightly warm, with just the hint of a breeze. Guy pulled the scent of pine and fresh air deep into his lungs, happy to finally be outside. The woods behind the apartment were thick and green; the sound of birds filled the tall trees. The sky, a deep blue, carried only a wisp of white clouds.

It wasn't as if he hadn't seen the beauty of nature before. In his work, especially when he made tourist runs, he saw it all the time. He just couldn't remember the last time he'd actually taken a moment to stop and appreciate that beauty. A long time, he realized as he spotted a moose and her calf watching him from the woods. A very long time.

He walked down a narrow alley between two buildings and came out onto a wooden sidewalk on the town's main street. Holly's store was flanked by

Grigsby's Hardware on the left and Mildred's Cut and Perm on the right. There was a sandwich shop and dentist office directly across the street and the usual array of quaint, small town shops up and down the two-lane road. There was a stop sign at the closest intersection, but no stoplight as far he could see.

He turned, looked through the large, plate-glass window of Holly's store, but didn't see her at the counter inside. A bell jangled when he opened the door, jangled again when he closed it. Still no one.

The store was small, with floor-to-ceiling shelves that seemed to carry a wide range of items. Clothing, dry and canned goods, assorted household items. A tidy display of scented candles on a table by the register counter caught his attention, and he picked one up to smell it. Lavender. The same candle that Holly kept in her bedroom on her nightstand. He'd found a strange comfort in that scent for the two days he'd slept in her bed and it made him smile now.

When still no one appeared, he strolled through the store, noticed several items made by native craftsmen and women: Aleutian baskets, brightly colored wool blankets, soft leather moccasins. He touched the corner of an embroidered red silk scarf and thought how pretty it would look draped around Holly's sexy neck. But he couldn't think about her neck without thinking about her mouth, couldn't help remembering what she'd tasted like, what her lips had felt like against his, the soft little sigh she'd made when he—

"Can I help you?"

He snatched his hand away from the scarf as if he'd been caught with his hand in the proverbial cookie jar. A woman stood behind him—late forties, streaks of silver in her springy brown hair. She wore a man's blue plaid flannel shirt and black trousers.

"Oh, heavens, I know who you are." She smiled and her entire face joined in. "You're that fellow Holly's been keeping upstairs. Folks in town were beginning to wonder if you really existed." She stuck out her hand. "Roberta Jones, but most folks just call me Bob."

Smiling, he took the woman's hand. She had a firm grip. "Guy Blackwolf."

"You're a handsome one," she said matter-of-factly as she looked him over. "And tall, too, like my second husband." Her brown eyes softened and she sighed. "Lord, I miss that man. All I've got to snuggle with now is George. He's not bad company, but keeps me up all night with that snoring of his."

Not sure if George was another husband or a dog, he simply said, "I was looking for Holly."

"Just missed her," Bob said. "She goes over to the school every Tuesday and Thursday afternoon. Nicholas or I watch the store for her while she's gone."

"Nicholas?"

"My youngest boy. He's only seventeen, but almost as tall as you. Trips over his own feet, though, especially when Holly's around."

"Is that right?"

"Last week she gave him a little peck on the cheek to thank him for fixing a squeaky door and the boy walked straight into a wall." Bob shook her head sadly. "You'd think after having five sons I'd understand the male species a little better."

Guy understood perfectly. If an older, gorgeous woman like Holly had kissed him when he'd been seventeen—even a little peck—he'd have walked into a wall, too. Even now, at thirty, he'd nearly had cardiac arrest, though the kiss they'd shared had been no little peck by any means. He wondered just how many more admirers she had in this town. Several, no doubt.

But this was hardly the time to be remembering that kiss. "Ah, is the school close to here?" he asked.

"You could hit it with a mean curveball," Bob said cheerfully. "Right around the corner, third building down, red brick. She'll be in the back room. Say, now that you're feeling better, why don't you come over and meet my boys and George? I make a mean chili and you could—"

The phone rang, cutting her off, and while she took the call, Guy grabbed a few items he needed and several more he didn't, including a handful of chocolate bars. The woman rang up the purchases while still on the phone, obviously arguing with one of her sons about using the truck Friday night. Guy quickly paid and headed out before she hung up.

He took his time on the short walk over, waved back at a battered green truck that drove by and gave a friendly honk. He felt the eyes on him from windows, saw the three women in the hair salon who rushed to the window and gawked at him, one with tiny curlers all over her head, another with some black goo on her hair. When he stopped and winked at them, their mouths dropped open.

He dug a chocolate bar out of his bag as he rounded the corner, unwrapped it, polished it off in four bites, then shoved the wrapper back into the bag as he stopped in front of the third building down. He frowned as he read the small wooden sign over the entry. Twin Pines School, Grades K-6.

What was Holly doing here?

She hadn't mentioned that she taught, but then, she hadn't mentioned anything about Bob or Nicholas, either. No doubt there were lots of things he didn't know about Holly Douglas. He wondered why that bothered him, why it mattered one way or the other how much he did or didn't know about her. Strangely, it did.

He went into the building, walked down the wide, polished green tile corridor to the back of the small building. The last door was opened halfway. Inside, someone was speaking. A child?

"'What do I want those silly shoes for? Zachary the Zebra said. I like my feet just fine the way they are. Those shoes will only slow me down, make it hard to skip through the meadow and run up the hills.'"

He peeked around the door. It wasn't a child speaking, Guy realized, though the voice was high-pitched like one. It was Holly. Her thick hair was swept up in a ponytail; she wore an emerald-green short-sleeved sweater and slim black jeans. On the floor in front of her, a dozen or so youngsters sat cross-legged, spellbound by her story.

Holly scanned her rapt audience as she deepened her voice. "'These shoes are called hooves, Zachary, and they will protect you, said Horatio the Hoofmaker. You'll still be able to skip and run, only faster.'"

Intrigued, Guy kept out of sight, watched as Holly told the story of Zachary, a zebra who lived in a time before zebras were born with hooves. Soon, Guy himself was as captivated as the children, hanging on Holly's every word, every gesture, every animated expression on her face as she told her story about a recalcitrant little zebra who was happy with his hoofless state and preferred to remain that way. Holly acted out the characters in the story, changing her voice and mannerisms to fit each one. A rhinoceros named Randy, an elephant named Elroy, and Andy the Anteater.

When Zachary lost the annual zebra race because he couldn't run as fast or as far as the other zebras, all the children frowned with disappointment. But when Zachary finally realized that he had no reason to be afraid of wearing his new hooves and leads the Animal Parade, all the children smiled with delight.

Guy smiled, too. So this was what she did on Tuesdays and Thursdays. Read to the kids here at the school. He had to admit she was terrific. She obviously enjoyed telling the stories as much as the children enjoyed hearing them. At the moment, they were all clapping and begging for more.

He watched her for a long moment while she laughed and spoke to the children, careful not to let her see him, not wanting to see the light in her eyes dim or her smile fade. Something he couldn't name shifted in his chest. His own smile faded.

She deserved to know the truth. He'd already waited longer than he should have to tell her. He'd told himself that he'd waited because she wasn't ready, that he hadn't prepared her, but the fact was that *he* hadn't been ready. He'd enjoyed spending time with her and hadn't wanted it to end just yet.

He stepped away from the door, though he could still hear the sound of her laughter from inside.

Tonight was the night.

All the way up the stairs and even as she opened the door to her apartment, Holly told herself that this time when she faced Mr. Guy Blackwolf, he would not ruffle her feathers. He would not get under her skin. He would not bother her in the slightest.

He would *not*.

Since he'd kissed her, she'd wasted way too much time and energy on the man. Two days worth. Two days of thinking about him, of constantly reliving that kiss, the way his mouth had felt on hers, the heat of his tongue against hers.

Two aggravating days wishing he would kiss her again, in spite of the fact that he'd rejected her.

But she was a big girl. Life went on, even if the man who'd finally made her toes curl and her skin sizzle didn't feel the same way she did. She'd learned how to survive disappointment in her life. Every frustration, every obstacle had made her a stronger, wiser woman.

She was calm now, composed. Indifferent.

Nothing was going to rattle her today. Nothing at all. She opened her front door, paused, then frowned.

What in the world was that strange screeching sound?

Her heart slammed against her ribs as a thin cloud of smoke circled her.

Oh dear Lord. The apartment was on fire!

"Guy!" Dropping her purse and the small bag of groceries in her hand, she rushed into her living room. "Guy!"

"What?"

His response, something between a snarl and a bark, came from the kitchen. Relief washed through her when she turned and saw him bent over her stove, enveloped in a cloud of smoke. At the moment, he was swearing like an angry truck driver.

He wore two cow pot-holder mitts on his hands and a white, ruffled apron around his waist.

Smoke billowed from the metal baking sheet he yanked from the oven. Muttering furiously under his breath, he stalked past her, tray in hand, and dumped it on her front porch.

He stalked back in, his face a tight mask of anger as hot as the burned—she glanced at the still smoking tray on her front porch—biscuits?

He jammed his pot-holdered fists on his lean hips and narrowed his eyes. "Don't say it. Not one word."

There was something about a six-foot-three, muscle-bound man in cow pot holders and a frilly apron that inspired laughter. But she didn't dare. Not with the murderous look he was giving her. Even a flicker of a smile might elicit death. So she pressed her lips together in a thin line, clasped her hands together and rocked back on the heels of her boots.

"I had everything under control." He jerked the mitts off his hands. "Your oven must be off."

"I'm sure that's it." She tried to keep her gaze level with his, she really did, but it was impossible not to glance down at the rumpled, food-splattered apron he still wore over his jeans. A spot of flour dusted his cheek and nose. She pressed a hand to her lips to cover her cough as well as the twitch in the corner of her mouth.

He glared at her, then yanked the apron off. "I made a macaroni and cheese casserole, too," he snapped. "If you have a chainsaw, we can cut it. And bring some straws for the chocolate pie while you're at it."

"What is all this?" she asked carefully.

"A thank you, that's what this is." With the smoke alarm still shrieking, he stomped to the kitchen, opened both windows. "It was supposed to be, anyway."

He did this for her? She followed him into the kitchen, looked at a baking bowl sitting on the countertop that contained the macaroni. At least, she *thought* it was macaroni.

She watched him wave the apron at the smoke like a flag of surrender. He really *had* done this for her, she realized. No man had ever made such a grand gesture for her before. It didn't matter that the meal he'd prepared was ruined. The attempt alone was enough to make her insides soft as warm butter.

"You didn't have to do this," she said over the

screech of the alarm, told herself that her eyes burned from the smoke, nothing else.

Muttering under his breath, he stood on a kitchen chair and disconnected the alarm, then climbed down again. With a sigh, he tossed the apron down on the kitchen table and faced her. "Yeah, I did. Not just to thank you, but to say I'm sorry."

Her pulse jumped when he moved close. "Sorry?"

The anger faded from his eyes as he glanced down at her. "You rattled me the other night, Holly. I'm not used to that."

"I rattled you?" She sounded like an idiot, repeating everything he said. But standing here, with those wolf eyes of his locked on hers, smoke swirling around them, she simply couldn't find her balance.

"You rattled me. Big time." He cupped her chin in his large hand. "I acted like a jerk."

"No." She didn't lean into him, but didn't pull away, either. "You were right. You were smart enough, responsible enough, to stop us both from heading down a dead-end street."

"Holly, I assure you, smart and responsible had absolutely nothing to do with me stopping." He sighed, dropped his hand away. "And now, I owe you a dinner, not to mention a new baking sheet. Get your coat, m'lady. We are going out."

The summer evening was pleasant, and they walked the two blocks to Twin Pines Lodge. In 1904 the original structure had been nothing more than a six-room log cabin, but over the past few decades, with asphalt roads and the ever-increasing word-of-mouth regarding the town's plentiful fishing and hunting, the lakeside lodge had continued to expand. There were fifty guest rooms now, a dining room that held up to one hundred patrons, and a fully staffed kitchen complete with a New York chef. The decorating scheme was mounted mooseheads, five-foot-long salmon and a variety of Alaskan artifacts. In the center of the dining room, hanging from a heavy, rough-cut timber beam, a kayak with two mannequins dressed like fishermen with paddles, seemed to float in midair. Candles in red glass holders flickered on the heavy pine tables.

After they ordered their meals and the waiter brought water and drinks, Guy raised his bottle of beer to Holly's glass of iced tea. "To restaurants."

"You might be sorry we came here," she said, tapping her glass to his bottle. "Now that there's been a Blackwolf sighting, everyone will be wanting a closer look. By tomorrow, the entire town will know that you ordered a Moosehead beer, Italian dressing on your salad and a porterhouse steak, medium rare."

Guy glanced around the room, saw several heads, male and female, turned in his and Holly's direction. So much for a quiet, intimate dinner. He *was* almost sorry he'd brought her out. After he told her why he'd come here, everything would be different between them. And tonight, if just for a little while, he'd wanted her for himself.

After they ate, he told himself, then he'd gently ease into why he was here. For the moment, he simply wanted to enjoy being with her.

"If you sit next to me and let me nibble on your neck," he teased, "we could spice up the gossip."

The flush of color on her cheeks pleased him as much as the thought of actually sinking his teeth into that smooth neck of hers.

"Nibble on a roll." She pushed the bread basket at him, then sipped at her tea. "I have enough spice in my life, thank you very much."

He had an overwhelming desire to taste her, with a smile on her lips and the ice-cold tea still on her tongue. He squelched the thought, took a long pull on his beer bottle. "Ah, yes. Bob told me about Nicholas. You sure you can handle that much spice?"

She frowned. "You met Bob?"

"This afternoon." Guy noticed two well-rounded women with identical Dutch Boy haircuts whispering and watching him from a nearby table. In fact, he realized, the women looked identical, too, except one wore a green sweater and the other red. Like Christmas, he thought, then turned his attention back to Holly. "She told me her son has a thing for you."

"Oh, for heaven's sake." Holly rolled her eyes. "He's seventeen. I'm sure he thinks I'm ancient."

"Darlin', that's the last thing that boy is thinking, and you certainly don't want to know what the first thing is."

"Nicholas is a sweet kid," she insisted. "And you have a dirty mind."

He shrugged, reached for a roll. "When a woman who looks like you walks into the room, every red-blooded male, seventeen or seventy, can't help but think about sex."

"If that's your idea of complimenting a woman, Blackwolf, you better rethink your technique." Still, her eyes glowed and the flush on her cheeks deepened. "We're in the twenty-first century now. Women like honesty and integrity, not empty flattery and sex-talk."

"So you wouldn't like it if I told you that you're the sexiest, most beautiful woman I've ever met?" He leveled his gaze at her. "And that I want you more than my next breath?"

She hesitated, met his gaze. "Not if you didn't mean it."

"What if I did mean it?" he asked quietly.

She went still. The moment hovered there between them, shimmered with possibility...

"Hello!"

Both Guy and Holly jumped at the loud, enthusiastic greeting. The Christmas Twins who'd been watching him stood beside the table.

"Sorry to bother you, Holly," the twin wearing green said. "We just wanted to say hi and remind you that you're bringing the punch for the fund-raiser on Saturday."

"Thank you, Lois." Holly smiled at the women. "I nearly forgot."

It was obvious to Guy that Holly hadn't forgotten at all, but she knew why the women had come over to the table. "Have you met Guy Blackwolf yet?" she asked.

The twins looked at him in tandem. "Why, no, we haven't," Red Twin said.

"Guy, this is Lois and Lilah Benthauser. Lois, Lilah, Guy Blackwolf."

The sisters' eyes disappeared when they smiled. In stereo, they said, "Hello, Guy."

"Ladies." He nodded, narrowed his eyes as he stared at them. "Have we met before?"

"We saw you through Mildred's window at the salon," Lois said, then exaggerated a wink at him. "Remember?"

Oh, yes. The women standing in the window he'd winked at. He couldn't help but grin at them. They were like two bubbles of energy ready to burst. "Of course I remember. Nice hair."

"Thank you." They both touched the sides of their new styles, then Lilah said solemnly, "We heard about your accident, you poor thing. Imagine, surviving a plane crash. You must be the luckiest man alive!"

"Well, I'm sitting here surrounded by three lovely ladies," he drawled, "so I guess I am pretty lucky."

The twins giggled. Holly rolled her eyes.

"Oh, you go on," Lois chirped and gave him a hearty poke on the shoulder with her finger. "I hope you're feeling well enough to come to the fund-raiser with Holly. You look like a man who knows how to dance."

"Not a step." He shook his head. "But maybe you ladies could show me one or two."

Wide-eyed, the twins looked at each other, then back at him. "We'd love to," Lilah said breathlessly. Lois nodded.

"Well, we'll leave you two to your dinner, then."

Lois waggled her fingers and Lilah followed suit. "See you Saturday, Guy. Holly."

When the twins were gone, Holly shook her head at him in disgust. "Here we are in the middle of summer, and I just witnessed the biggest snow job I've ever seen."

"What?" He clasped a hand to his chest. "What did I do?"

"You know exactly—"

Their food came at that moment, effectively cutting her off. After the waiter left, she leaned close and whispered loudly, "That's exactly the kind of blarney I've been talking about. 'I guess I am pretty lucky,'" she mimicked him in a Goofy voice. "'And golly, gee, maybe you ladies could teach me how to dance.'"

"Why, Holly, I do believe you're jealous." He dug into his steak. "I had no idea you cared. Don't worry, I'll save a dance for you, too. Why don't you tell me what the fund-raiser is for?"

She closed her eyes in exasperation, opened them again on a sigh. "The school. We're too small to be subsidized by the state, and we don't want our children to ride in buses two hours every day to go to the next closest school."

"So the town pays on their own?"

She nodded, took a bite of her salad. "A lot of people help out. Teaching, bringing food in, cleaning up."

"Reading to the kids?"

She glanced up sharply.

"I saw you today. At the school with the kids."

"Well." She leaned back, arched a brow. "You certainly had a busy day."

"You were great." He watched her eyes narrow in distrust at his compliment. "No snow job, Holly. No blarney. I mean it. You were terrific. The kids were all crazy about you."

And I was, too, he almost said, but caught himself in time. He wasn't crazy *about* her, he told himself. But he just might be crazy *for* her.

"I'm crazy about them, too," she said, cutting off his wayward thoughts. "They're all so innocent, so sweet and trusting. They give me so much more than I give them."

"What do they give you?"

"Something to believe in," she said quietly as she stared at the chicken on her plate. "A renewal of faith in mankind. Unconditional love."

That was a big order to fill, Guy thought, surprised at the intensity in her voice. "Why haven't you married the local lumberjack and settled down with little lumberjacks and lumberjills of your own?"

"I intend to." She shrugged. "But only when it's right."

Guy had the oddest sensation of something tightening around his neck. "And how will you know when it's right?"

"I'll know." She pushed the butter around inside her baked potato, then took a bite. "What about you? Why haven't you taken the plunge?"

"Not me." He shook his head. "I'm up in the air more than I'm on the ground, and kids are one of life's mysteries to me. A terrifying mystery, at that."

She laughed softly. "You're a mystery, Blackwolf. Every time I think I've got you figured out, you take a sharp turn. Who are you really?"

He'd wanted to wait until later to tell her, let her finish her meal and enjoy the evening. But he couldn't. He knew he had to tell her now. "Holly, there's—"

Suddenly Keegan was standing there, beside the table. Guy felt the heat of his glare.

"I'll tell you who he is, Holly," Keegan said tightly. "He's a fraud."

Six

"**K**eegan, what are you talking about?" Holly stared at the man, who was currently in a stare-down with Guy.

"Ask him." Keegan nodded at Guy. "Ask him what he's really doing here in Twin Pines. Why he came here."

"He was delivering supplies." She had no idea what was going on, but as she glanced from Keegan to Guy, saw the tight set of Guy's jaw and the narrowing of his eyes, she had a bad feeling.

A very bad feeling.

"I just spoke with Andy, a pilot who works for Pelican in Seattle," Keegan said evenly. "Turns out Andy was the pilot scheduled to make that run, but your friend here paid him to trade."

"Pilots trade runs all the time," she said. "Why does that mean anything?"

"By itself, it doesn't." Keegan's voice still had an edge to it, but his face softened when he turned to her. "But Guy asked specifically about you, Holly, before he suggested the trade. About Holly Douglas. Told Andy that you were a friend of a friend."

"Holly." Guy dragged his gaze from Keegan. "I can explain."

Holly turned stiffly toward Guy. "Go ahead."

Guy shot a vicious look at Keegan. "Alone."

And then she knew. She knew exactly why he was here, and she knew exactly who had sent him. There was only one person who would go to all this trouble.

Ryan Fortune.

The dinner she'd been enjoying only a moment before now felt like a lump of cement in her stomach.

"Keegan." Holly kept her voice even and controlled. "Would you mind? I need to speak to Mr. Blackwolf."

Keegan balked. "I'm not leaving you alone with this—"

His hands clenched into fists, Guy started to rise.

"Sit back down," Holly hissed through her clenched teeth. Guy hesitated, kept his hot gaze on Keegan, then did as she asked. Holly placed a reassuring hand on Keegan's arm. "I'll be fine, Keegan. I know why he's here. I'll explain later."

A muscle worked in Keegan's jaw as he glanced back at Guy, but then he nodded. "I'll call you."

When he was gone, Holly drew in a slow breath

and locked her gaze onto Guy. "How much did Ryan and Miranda Fortune pay you to come here?"

He shook his head. "It's not like that, Holly." Guy kept his voice low as he leaned forward. "I was going to tell you tonight."

"Really?" Icy sarcasm edged her tone. "Before or after you got me into bed? That's been the plan all along, hasn't it? Let me think I could trust you, take me out for a little food and conversation, tell me how beautiful I am, how sexy, then whisk me back to my apartment for a quick roll in the—"

"Dammit, stop that," he said louder than he should. Several heads turned their way. He exhaled sharply, then sat back in his seat and said quietly, "I came to Twin Pines to talk to you, that's all."

If this discussion escalated any further, Holly realized, it would be all over town tomorrow that they were sleeping together and had a lover's spat right in the middle of the Twin Pines Lodge dining room. If they weren't in a public place with all these people around, she'd rip his liver out right now and serve it to him on his plate.

Instead she smiled, laughed casually for all the eyes that were on them.

"Fine." She snapped the word out from under her breath while she held her smile in place. "We'll talk. But not here."

She stood as if nothing at all had happened, when inside her blood was boiling. Calmly, casually, smiling and saying hello to the people she knew, she walked out of the restaurant ahead of Guy while he paid the bill.

She was nearly halfway back to her apartment by the time he caught up with her. She kept her strides long and quick and her gaze straight ahead. "I should have let you drown."

"Will you slow down and let me talk?"

"No." He took hold of her arm, but she yanked it away and kept walking. Her boots clomped on the wooden sidewalk. "You had no right to come here. No right at all. I came to Twin Pines to put as much distance between myself and the Fortune family as I possibly could. They have no place here. This is *my* place. *My* home."

Fists swinging at her sides, she stomped up the stairs to her apartment, then marched into her kitchen. He followed her inside and closed the front door. When he moved toward her, she put out a hand, palm up and he stopped.

"They just want to meet you, Holly."

"No. *N. O.*, no. I already told Ryan and Miranda Fortune I want no part of their family."

"Their brother, Cameron, was your father, Holly," Guy said gently. "That makes the Fortunes your family, too."

"Just because the bastard jumped in every available bed in the state of Texas and got who knows how many women pregnant before he moved on to the next doesn't make him a father any more than it makes his family mine." She slammed one open window shut, then moved to the next, but it stuck. Frustrated, furious, she pulled harder.

"Let me do that."

"Just keep away." She struggled with the window. "Haven't you done enough?"

"I'm sorry I didn't tell you right away," he said. "But after the crash, I just needed a little time. Not just to get my strength back, but to give you time to know me, to know that I didn't come here to hurt you."

"Mister, I don't know you at all." She slammed her fist on the top of the window and pain radiated up her arm. It felt good, she thought, preferred it to the pain in her heart. But still the window refused to budge. "And lies always hurt, Blackwolf. Men like you, like my father, don't quite get that concept."

He grabbed hold of her shoulders, turned her around and brought his face within inches of hers. "Don't you compare me to Cameron Fortune," he said in a low, dangerous tone. "I may not be proud of everything I've done in my life, but I would never, *ever* abandon a child." He dropped his hands and stepped back. "You got that?"

She wasn't prepared for the onslaught of raw emotion that spilled from his body into hers, or for her reaction to it. Her arms burned where he'd touched her; her insides sizzled. The faint smell of smoke still hung in the air, but she wasn't sure if it was from the earlier oven disaster, or from herself.

But she did know that she believed him. If not about other things, then about this one thing. Her acceptance of that fact, that he would never abandon a child, somehow took the heat out of her anger.

"I never met him once when he was alive." She stepped back against the wall, rubbed at her arms where his touch had scorched her. "Why the hell should I care about him now that he's dead?"

"This isn't about Cameron Fortune." He turned away and to her annoyance, easily closed the window. "This is about you. You have half sisters, half brothers, aunts and uncles and cousins."

She shook her head. "I want nothing to do with Cameron Fortune's family. That part of my life is closed. I have no intention of opening it up again."

"They're your family, Holly." He sighed, raked a hand through his hair. "They just want to meet you."

"Not interested. My store, my life, is here in Twin Pines now. I'm not interested in their money, their power or their prestige. There's nothing they can give me, or I can give them. You wasted a trip here, Blackwolf, not to mention a perfectly good airplane. But then I suppose Ryan and Miranda Fortune have more than enough money to buy you a hundred planes in addition to your fee." She brushed past him. "Now if you'll excuse me, I'm going to bed. The couch is yours tonight, but I want you out of here tomorrow."

"Holly."

She paused, glanced over her shoulder at him.

"Believe whatever you want, but the Fortunes didn't pay me to come here. I came here as a favor to a friend. And what happened between us—" he leveled his gaze with hers "—had nothing to do with the Fortunes."

"Nothing happened between us, Guy," she said, felt the emptiness of the truth in that statement. "Nothing."

When she closed the bedroom door behind her, she

laid her cheek against the cool wood and blinked back
the threatening tears.

Absolutely nothing at all.

Two a.m. came, but not sleep. Guy sat on the
couch, stared into the darkness as he wrestled between
pounding on Holly's bedroom door or just simply
leaving. He had no idea where he'd go if he left, or
where he'd sleep, but what the hell, he wasn't sleeping anyhow.

He got up, reached for his bag, then swore and sat
back down.

He couldn't leave. Not yet. He and Holly weren't
finished. Not by a long shot.

Lord, but he'd made a mess of this. He had no idea
how to make it right, but he knew he had to try. Not
just for his sake, but for Holly's. She'd saved his life
and he repaid her by hurting her. And while an apol-
ogy certainly wouldn't make everything hunky-dory,
it was the only place he knew where to start.

He couldn't even be angry at Keegan. He'd been
watching out for Holly, protecting her, which was
more than he could say for himself. He didn't have
to like the man to respect him.

He got up again and this time headed for the bedroom. And stopped.

Oh, hell.

With a heavy sigh, he raked both hands through his
hair, then went into the kitchen and flipped on the
light over the stove. He'd already cleaned up the mess
he'd made earlier, but the cold, hard lump of macaroni and cheese he'd attempted to make still sat in a

bowl on the counter. He had no idea what to do with it, though he thought it might make a good anchor. No doubt Holly would love to cram the concoction, bowl and all, down his throat.

He stared at the bowl, then suddenly went still.

He felt her presence before he actually heard her. When he turned, she stood in the dim light of the kitchen doorway, her hands jammed deep into the pockets of a blue robe, watching him with her cool cat eyes. Her hair fell around her shoulders in a wild mass of chestnut curls. Hair a man could drag his hands through.

His hands fisted at the thought; he pushed the image out of his mind. The last thing in the world she wanted was for him to touch her, let alone all the other things he'd fantasized since the first moment he'd opened his eyes and she'd been standing over him.

So he stood still, waited, heard the sound of his own heartbeat in the quiet and the soft hoot of an owl in the woods behind her apartment.

"What kind of pie did you say you made?" she said after a long moment that felt more like hours rather than seconds.

He frowned. "What?"

"You said earlier that you'd made a pie." She moved a little closer, wary, but without the anger that she'd stormed out with earlier. "What kind?"

"Chocolate." He opened the refrigerator, pulled out the pie and held it up as an offering. It was lop-sided, but didn't look too bad. "With whipped cream.

Do you want to eat it,'' he asked carefully, ''or throw it in my face?''

One corner of her mouth turned up. ''I'll have to taste it first to decide which will give me more satisfaction.''

A truce, he realized, felt a wave of relief pour through him. He'd been prepared to crawl if necessary—Lord knew she deserved a little groveling—but she was waving a white flag.

Would she ever cease to amaze him?

She pulled two plates from the cupboard, a pie cutter and spoons out of the drawer, then set them on the table. He gave up trying to slice the pie and spooned it onto the plates instead. Even in the dim light he could see the amusement in her eyes as she looked at the lumpy mound of chocolate pudding.

Her first bite was as small as it was tentative. ''Not bad. What's this crust made out of?''

''Vanilla wafers.'' He took a bite himself and decided it was edible, after all. ''My sister used to make it for me on special occasions.''

''What kind of special occasions?''

It was small talk. But the fact she was talking to him at all was a miracle. ''Birthdays. If I'd make it through a week without cutting school or having the principal call. If my dad made it home from work in time for dinner. That was a real special occasion.''

There was something about sitting at a kitchen table with a woman, in the semidark, in the middle of the night, eating chocolate cream pie, that felt... comfortable. A kind of comfortable he'd never felt before.

"And your mother?"

He shrugged. "She was Italian, with huge brown eyes and a smile that turned men to drooling idiots." He scooped a bite of pudding onto his spoon. "I was eleven when she decided that life with a traveling rock band was more interesting than a half-breed bench press operator and two kids. My dad took it hard."

"And you?" Holly asked quietly. "Did you take it hard?"

He shrugged. "I had my sister, Susan. She was four years older and ran the house like a drill sergeant." He hadn't thought about those days in a very long time, Guy realized. "After she graduated nursing school, she told everyone she was going to get married and have six children, two dogs and three cats."

"Did she?"

"No." He stared at the pie on his plate. Susan's had always been perfect. He wished he'd paid closer attention when she'd tried to teach him how to cook. "She died when she was twenty-four. Breast cancer. Seems she took care of everyone but herself."

Holly drew in a slow breath, then let it out. "Oh, Guy, I'm so sorry."

"It was a long time ago." Sometimes it felt like a hundred years, other times, like last week. "She went to school with Flynn Sinclair."

She glanced up. "The same Flynn Sinclair who sent me an invitation to the Fortune family get-together several months ago?"

He nodded, watched her expression turn from sad

to surprise. "He was there for Susan through everything," Guy said evenly.

"So he's the friend you did a favor for." She studied him thoughtfully in the dim light. "The reason you came here."

"Yes. Look, Holly—" he pushed his plate away and leaned toward her "—I talked to Flynn today. He told me that your uncle's in the hospital. They don't know what's wrong with him, but they're running tests. Your Aunt Miranda asked if you would at least call."

He saw the hesitation in her eyes, then she shook her head slowly. "Guy, I'm sorry the man is ill, but it doesn't change anything for me. I'm also sorry you came all this way for nothing. The Fortune name means nothing more to me than memories of long, cold winters when my mother didn't have enough money to heat the tiny trailer we lived in. Or the hand-me-downs I wore growing up that the other kids made fun of, the birthday parties I could never go to. The boys I never dated or brought home because my mother would most likely be passed out on the sofa because alcohol was the only thing that eased the ache in her heart for a man who never gave a damn about her."

"Cameron Fortune was a first class bastard and irresponsible fool." *Just for starters,* Guy thought. "But maybe before you lump his family in the same category, you should at least give them a chance."

"Why should I give them a chance?" She stood, turned her back as she moved to the window and stared stiffly out into the night. "Because some of the

Fortune blood runs in my veins? It takes a lot more than that to make a family.''

He came behind her, shoved his hands into his pockets to keep from touching her. ''You're right. It takes people who care about you, who are there for you when you need them, who accept you exactly as you are. People you can argue with and get mad at, but you never walk away from.''

She shook her head. ''If you think I want that with the Fortunes, or that I need it, you're wrong. I've done without them for twenty-six years, Guy, and I'm doing just fine.''

''Are you?''

Eyes narrowed and lips pressed tight, she turned to face him. ''You can't just waltz into my life for a few days and think you know me. You don't know what I want or what I think or what I feel.''

''Maybe not,'' he said calmly. ''But tell me you haven't ever wondered if maybe one of your cousins or an aunt has the same eyes as you do, or the same color hair. Maybe the same voice. If they all sit around a big table of food at Thanksgiving or Christmas and laugh and talk. Tell me that you've never wondered, even once, if just maybe there was a seat at that table for you.''

''No.''

He smiled. ''There's one thing you don't do well, Holly, and that's lie. Your eyes give you away every time.''

''Maybe you could give me some lessons,'' she said, lifting her chin.

''I deserve that,'' he said tightly. ''But don't let

your feelings for me keep you from finding out the truth. It's easier to regret having done something, than to regret not doing it and wishing you had."

"Is it?" she asked quietly.

Her gaze held steady on his, then slowly slid to his mouth. His pulse leaped; heat raced through his veins.

Just like that. A simple look and he felt the need, felt himself harden. He wanted.

Thankful he had his hands in his pockets, he stepped away. If he touched her now, if he took her in his arms, there'd be no stopping. Emotions were too high, too raw, and he'd be taking advantage of that if they went to bed together. He knew that if they did make love, she'd only despise him in the morning.

It took every ounce of willpower he possessed not to close the distance between them, not to drag his hands through that wild hair of hers and take what he knew she was offering.

When he kept his distance, the desire he'd seen in her eyes faded. The hollow, empty look he now saw clawed at his insides.

She turned from him, shoved her own hands into the pockets of her robe as she looked out the window. "So maybe I have wondered," she said, her voice almost a whisper. "On birthdays, or the swim meet when I took first place for high dive. My high school graduation. Christmas Eve. Those were the times it hurt the most. When I envied the other kids as much as I hated my own mother for not loving me as much as the man who'd abandoned us both."

"Holly—"

"You can stay here until the insurance adjuster

comes in, but only on the condition you don't mention the Fortunes again.''

He sighed, then nodded. "Fair enough."

"That's more than fair, Blackwolf. But I figure since I'm the reason you're here, I can at least give you a place to sleep for a few more nights."

"Thanks."

She brushed past him, paused at the doorway, then said quietly, "Ryan and Miranda Fortune are going to have to accept that I'm not going back to Texas, and so are you. There's nothing for me there. There never was, and there never will be."

He watched her go, heard the soft click of her bedroom door as it closed behind her, and wondered if she really believed that.

Seven

The annual Twin Pines School fund-raiser was *the* summer event. Locals, as well as people from all the neighboring towns, filled the large community center building. This year's theme was Italian; the scent of oregano and garlic filled the cool, summer night air, along with the mouthwatering smells of bubbling marinara and ricotta-filled lasagna. Lively conversations and laughter mixed with the sound of a live band playing the theme song from *The Godfather*.

Holly took in the room and couldn't help but smile. Red-checkered tablecloths, flickering candles, carafes of Chianti. All they needed to complete the picture was Marlon Brando and Al Pacino. When her gaze swept the room and came to rest on Guy, who was speaking to Ed Burton, Twin Pines postmaster, the smile on her lips faded.

Play The *Lucky Hearts* Game

and get...

FREE BOOKS & a FREE GIFT... YOURS to KEEP!

Yes! I have scratched off the silver card. Please send me my **2 FREE BOOKS** and **FREE MYSTERY GIFT**. I understand that I am under no obligation to purchase any books as explained on the back of this card.

Scratch Here!
then look below to see
what your cards get you.

326 SDL DC56   **225 SDL DC5Z**

NAME   (PLEASE PRINT CLEARLY)

ADDRESS

APT.#   CITY

STATE/PROV.   ZIP/POSTAL CODE

Twenty-one gets you
2 FREE BOOKS and a
FREE MYSTERY GIFT!

Twenty gets you
2 FREE BOOKS!

Nineteen gets you
1 FREE BOOK!

TRY AGAIN!

Offer limited to one per household and not valid to current Silhouette Desire® subscribers. All orders subject to approval.

Visit us online at
www.eHarlequin.com

(S-D-OS-09/01)   DETACH AND MAIL CARD TODAY!

She told herself this wasn't a date. Or anything that even resembled a date. For the past four days, since that night in her kitchen, they'd barely even seen each other. Guy had spent most of his time down at the garage with Quincy and she'd been in meetings nearly every night with Lois and Lilah, the chairpersons for the fund-raiser. When Guy had volunteered his services to help out tonight, she could hardly turn him down. It was, after all, for the kids. Just because she and Guy had walked over here together, didn't mean that they were "together."

Still, as she watched Janet Mercer join Ed and Guy, then turn her baby-blue eyes on Guy, Holly's fingers tightened around her glass of punch. The blonde, thirty-three-year-old divorcée was constantly on the prowl and no doubt she thought that Guy would make a handsome addition to her ever-growing list of bedroom trophies. When Janet laughed and leaned forward, her breasts threatened to overflow from the plunging neckline of her yellow blouse. Her leather skirt was tight, black and short, her heels high. With the black choker around her neck, Holly thought she looked like a bumblebee.

"Damn, but that's one fine-looking man."

Holly nearly spilled her punch at the unexpected comment from behind her. Holding a paper plate laden with antipasto, Bob moved beside her and stared at the trio across the room.

"I suppose so," Holly said with what she hoped was a bored tone. Actually she thought Guy looked devastating. The charcoal-gray long-sleeved shirt he'd bought today deepened the gray of his eyes, and the black slacks fit over his bottom like a hug. Holly shrugged, then said facetiously, "If you like the ruggedly handsome, incredibly charming with a dash of dangerous, type."

"Funny," Bob said thoughtfully as she popped an olive into her mouth. "I never thought of Ed that way."

"Oh." Holly felt her cheeks warm. "I thought you were talking about…I mean, I thought—"

Bob grinned. "Just kidding. Everyone knows that Ed is a fine postmaster, but the poor man must have been out to lunch when the Good Lord passed out looks. But speaking of looks—" Bob looked her up and down "—you clean up real nice, honey. Something new?"

"Not really." Holly had seen the black silk slip dress in a catalog and though she hadn't been able to afford it and couldn't imagine where she'd ever wear such a thing, she still couldn't resist buying it. The dress had sat in her closet for almost a year, so technically, it wasn't new, but she hadn't worn it before, either.

She hadn't planned on wearing it tonight, either. She'd already put on a simple white cotton T and long floral skirt when the black dress whispered to her, *"Me, wear me."* It *was* silly for the dress to just hang there, after all. But she wasn't wearing it for anybody but herself, she thought firmly as her gaze drifted back to Guy.

She'd just wanted to look nice. That's all. Wanted to feel good about herself. That late-night chat with Guy had stirred up a lot of old feelings that she'd thought she'd long overcome. Feelings of inadequacy and being "less than." Of being different from everyone else and never fitting in.

Feelings of rejection.

And Lord knew, on top of all that, what little confidence she'd had regarding her appeal to the opposite sex had been smashed to smithereens by Guy. When they'd stood in the dim light of her kitchen the other night, after she'd called a truce between them, she'd thought she'd seen something in his eyes. Something that had nothing to do with the Fortunes, and everything to do with whatever was happening between them. She'd wanted him to kiss her, had practically asked him to.

But he hadn't. So once again she'd been wrong.

Still, when she'd come out of the bedroom this evening in this dress, there'd been a look of male appreciation in his gaze. A slow head-to-toe sweep of her body with those wolf eyes of his that had made her skin tingle with anticipation. Then he'd looked away and the moment passed as if it had never happened.

So obviously, nothing had happened, currently was happening, or was going to happen between them.

"Have a heart," Bob said.

"What?" Holly glanced at the woman.

"Artichoke heart." She held her plate up to Holly.

"Oh. Thanks. Maybe just a pickle."

Bob stared curiously as Holly took a bite. "So you wanna tell me about it?"

"About what?" Holly frowned as two women from her book club, Elma Johnson and Helen Lindsey, joined the growing circle of females around Guy.

Both single, attractive women who'd recently come to Alaska after hearing there was an abundance of available men. Holly liked them both.

So why did she have a sudden urge to scratch their eyes out?

"Holly."

"Hmm?" She looked back at Bob.

"You're eating an avocado with the skin still on."

Holly stopped chewing, grimaced as she realized what she'd done. Yuck. "I always eat them this way." To prove it, she continued to chew. "Lots of vitamins and minerals in the skin."

Smiling, Bob handed Holly a napkin. "Lord Almighty, you do have it bad, don't you?"

Holly delicately spit the hard skin into the napkin, then took a sip of her punch. "I have no idea what you're talking about."

"Have it your way, honey." Bob shrugged. "But I've had three husbands and five sons. I know a few things about the birds and the bees. And girl—" she popped a square of cheese into her mouth, then looked over her shoulder as she walked away "—you've been stung."

Ridiculous, Holly thought. So maybe she did think Guy was sexy and maybe she was attracted to him. So what? That certainly didn't mean that she "had it bad" or she'd been "stung."

The only thing that had been "stung" when it came to Guy Blackwolf was her pride and she could live with that.

He'd be leaving next week. An insurance adjuster was flying in on Wednesday to check out the damages to Guy's plane, and though he hadn't said so, Holly knew that he'd go back to Seattle with the man. He had no reason to stay.

She took another sip of punch. No reason at all.

When she glanced back at him, she noticed that Ed Burton had left, but the circle of admirers around Guy had grown to five or six women. No doubt he was charming them all with grand stories of his life as a daring bush pilot. Describing his crash into the lake, in elaborate detail, and how he'd escaped the icy fingers of death's hand.

The conversation was certainly animated, she thought, annoyed with herself that she was interested at all. Guy was adamantly shaking his head, while Elma and the assistant manager at the lodge, Linda Thornton, were nose-to-nose in a heated debate.

In spite of herself, she wandered through the sea of people in the large room until she was close enough to hear.

"She saved his life, didn't she?" Elma was saying to Linda. "He'd be dead if it wasn't for her. Have you forgotten that?"

Holly froze. They were talking about *her?*

Linda pointed a finger at Elma. "Of course not. But that doesn't mean she can just rip his heart out of his chest and stomp on it."

I haven't ripped out anyone's heart, Holly thought and stared in disbelief at Guy's broad back. What was he telling these women?

"She's coldhearted," Guy jumped in and Holly nearly gasped. "An Alaskan storm has more warmth than that woman."

Oh, is that so? Narrowing her eyes, she moved closer. Maybe she *would* rip out his heart and stomp on it, she decided.

Linda turned on Elma. "She loves him. Anybody with half a brain can see that. Why can't she just tell him the truth?"

Holly pressed a hand to her mouth. She *didn't* love him. What was the matter with everyone? An infatuation maybe, a preoccupation, but *love?* She'd hardly call that love.

She was opening her mouth to set the record straight when Helen piped up, "How can she tell him the truth now, after the doctors told her she can never have children? She knows that he wants more children. It's because she loves him that she lied to him."

Confused, Holly simply stood there, mouth still open, and stared. The doctors never told me I can't have children, she thought. What in the *world* were they all talking about?

"Hey, if you ask me, Gerald's getting a raw deal," Guy said. "I say he walks away now and cuts his losses."

"Victoria dragged him from a burning building," Helen said in the woman's defense. "Why can't he see she loves him?"

Guy shook his head. "Hey, Gerald can't read Victoria's mind. She needs to tell him what she wants and let him make his own decision."

Guy's comment created a flurry of discussion between the circle. Holly watched in stunned amazement.

They were talking about a soap opera, for heaven's

sake. She rolled her eyes, relieved that the conversation hadn't been about her. So *that's* what he did with his afternoons, she thought, shaking her head as a slow smile curved her lips. Watched *Storm's Cove.* The man was unbelievable.

She moved in, slipped her arm in his and smiled at the other women. "Mind if I borrow him for a little while?" she asked sweetly. "Guy promised to sell Bingo cards at the raffle booth."

There were groans of disappointment and several looks of longing from the women, but reluctantly, they relinquished him to Holly.

"Once again I owe my life to you." He leaned close to speak quietly into her ear as they walked away. "It was getting ugly there."

"My thoughts exactly. But I wasn't trying to save you. I was saving the women."

"What's that supposed to mean?" His eyes widened with innocence.

"Never mind." She patted his hand. "Are you hungry?"

"Starving." His gaze slid over her, and if only for a moment, that look—the same look he'd given her when he'd first seen her in this dress—was there again. A look of hunger that had nothing to do with food. She had to remind herself to breathe.

The band started a new song, something soft and sexy and slow.

"We should do something about that," she murmured.

"Absolutely."

Her breath caught when he pulled her into his arms,

and the heat of his narrowed gaze shot like an arrow straight down to her toes. Without warning, he spun her. She gasped at the unexpected move, then suddenly found herself on the dance floor with the other couples.

When he eased her body close to hers, her pulse raced.

"I wasn't talking about dancing." But she held on, slid her arms up his shoulders and marveled at the feel of solid muscle under the soft cotton of his shirt.

"Neither was I."

Dammit, why did this have to feel so good? Holly thought. All those nights, lying in her bed, knowing he was only a few feet away, she'd wondered what it would feel like to take it to the next level from the kiss they'd shared. Wondered what his hands would feel like on her, his mouth, his body. Bare skin to bare skin.

She breathed in the masculine scent of him, a blend of soap and aftershave as fresh as the Alaskan woods. When his clean-shaven chin brushed her temple, pleasure rippled across her skin.

No man had ever made her knees weak and her hands tremble. Made her ache with a need she didn't understand. She'd felt physical attraction before, but nothing like this, nothing that even came close. Every feeling she'd ever had for a man paled next to Guy. Like a firecracker next to a keg of dynamite.

Why now? she thought in despair. Why did she have to feel this now, for this man, when they could never go anywhere, except maybe the bedroom. She'd planned her life carefully, knew exactly what she wanted, where she was going and how she would get there. It would be risky, as well as dangerous, if she strayed from that road.

She could be strong when she needed to be, she told herself firmly. When he pulled her body flush with his and slid his hand to the small of her back, when she wanted nothing more than to melt into him and give herself up to every feeling, every sensation, she knew this was definitely a moment that required strength.

She didn't melt, but she didn't pull away, either.

"So it's soap operas, is it?" She forced her tone to be light.

"WWF and boxing don't come on in the afternoon," he defended. "And besides, *Storm's Cove* is a well-written daytime drama that clearly demonstrates the human condition."

She arched a brow. "What condition is that?"

Smiling, he wiggled his brows. "Sex and lust, of course. What else?" He twirled her a half-turn, then dipped her. "Did I mention how captivating you look this evening, my dear?"

She laughed at his foolishness, told herself that the compliment didn't mean a thing, that she only felt warm from the physical activity of dancing. "Next thing I know you'll be asking for bonbons and reading *Life With Marcy Pruitt.*"

"Now there's a fine woman to catch a man's eye." He twirled her again, guided her through the other couples to the middle of the floor.

She missed a step. "Are you telling me that you read *Life With Marcy Pruitt?*" The monthly magazine was mostly cooking and crafts and sewing. Definitely not the kind of reading material that Holly would imagine a burly bush pilot sitting down with.

"No, I don't read the magazine, but I've seen pictures of the woman. She's hot. And Helen told Elma that there's a how-to article this month on decorating pushpins and a recipe for homemade whole-wheat crackers. Now there's a woman a man could come home to at night."

"Marcy Pruitt?" The woman might be famous for her creme brulé or homemade party favors, but hot? "Are we talking about the same woman? Horn-rimmed glasses, Dutch boy haircut, too shy for public appearances?"

"That's the one. Those glasses are sexy."

"Now I know you're putting me on."

"Am I?"

He'd whispered the two words in her ear and the warmth of his breath made her heart skip. It took every ounce of willpower not to close her eyes and lean her head on his strong shoulder. When his hand dipped lower on her back, waves of heat coursed through her veins.

It was difficult to say exactly when the mood between them changed from teasing to serious, but one minute he was grinning and his eyes were laughing, the next minute, his gaze turned to smoke and his smile slowly faded. And neither one of them were thinking about Marcy Pruitt and her decorated push-pins.

His hand tightened at her waist. "Holly—"

"Guy Blackwolf, you're a big, fat fibber!"

Startled, both Guy and Holly turned. Lois and Lilah, arms folded, stood watching.

"Why, you can so dance," Lois said, but it was a cheerful accusation. "May I cut in, Holly? Lilah and I tossed a coin and I get to go first."

Smiling, Holly stepped out of his arms, not certain if she was relieved or disappointed. "He's all yours, Lois." Holly's heart was still pounding against her ribs when she leaned down and whispered in Lois's ear. "Watch out, though, the man's hands tend to roam."

Lois's eyes widened at Holly's warning, and so did her smile. She nearly knocked Guy over as she threw her arms around him. Guy glanced at Holly, an imploring look in his eyes, but she simply smiled back and walked away. At the edge of the dance floor, Lilah waited impatiently for her turn.

When Holly spoke to the band leader and requested the next song be another slow one, he was happy to oblige.

Suddenly famished, she headed for the pasta table. It was about time that Guy Blackwolf got his comeuppance.

Three hours later, when he saw Lois and Lilah, necks craned as they searched over the heads of the still crowded dance floor, Guy slipped out the back door of the community center onto a covered patio. He liked the two ladies well enough, and he hadn't minded dancing with them a few times, but enough was enough already. One more giggle, one more,

"Oh, you!" and he thought he just might have to jump back into the lake Holly had pulled him out of.

Outside, flames crackled in a patio fire pit, and the scent of pine and woodsmoke filled the cool night air. There were small groups of men and women standing around, laughing and talking, and though he nodded at a few people he'd been introduced to during the course of the evening, he kept walking. Inside the community center, the band played a hip-moving fast number and the Bingo barker shouted B-4.

Guy followed a steep river rock stairway leading from the patio down to a stand of young cedars that overlooked the lake. Light from a full moon shimmered on the water like liquid silver. Bass boats moored off a small dock bobbed gently with each tiny rolling wave.

About as far from Texas as a person could get.

Which was exactly why Holly had come here, Guy thought. To leave old, painful memories behind and start a new life.

But had she? he wondered. Or had she simply packed up all those memories and feelings and brought them along with her?

He'd had just that one dance with her, then she'd managed to avoid him the rest of the evening. He'd seen her serving lasagna and pasta at one point, smiling and laughing at everyone as they'd moved through the food line. Then he'd seen her dancing with Keegan, smiling and laughing with him, as well. That had put him in a bad mood.

Dammit, he wanted her in *his* arms, smiling and laughing at *him.* Since she'd walked out of the bedroom earlier wearing that slinky black dress and those high heels, her lips red and tiny pearls at her earlobes, he'd been a goner. Not a minute, not a second had passed all evening that he hadn't thought about her. That he hadn't wanted her.

"Beautiful, isn't it?"

Startled, he turned at the sound of her voice. She stood a few feet away, staring out across the lake.

"Stunning," he said, keeping his eyes on her.

She moved into the stand of cedars, slid her arms behind her back as she leaned against one wide trunk. "Three years ago, when I first came here and saw all this, it didn't seem real to me," she said quietly. "It felt like that movie where the town and its people were all phony, sets and actors created to fool the main character."

"The Truman Show?"

She nodded. "But it wasn't that way at all, of course. These people and this place is more real, more honest than anything I've ever known." Her gaze wandered to the lake's shoreline where a line of ducklings quietly swam behind their mother. "I found something here I'd never known before."

Her eyes had a dreamy quality to them that made Guy's chest tighten. "What did you find?"

"Myself." She turned her head toward him, smiled. "I found me."

He moved beside her, watched the silver moonlight shimmer in her golden eyes. "And who is that?" he asked.

She shrugged. "A woman not so different from any other."

"And that surprised you? That you were like other women?"

"Yes." Embarrassed, her gaze dropped to the ground. "I know it's silly."

"I didn't say it was silly." Because it was impossible not to touch her, he took her chin in his hand and lifted her face. "But I'm not sure I understand why you would want to be like anybody else when you're so right just exactly the way you are."

Her skin was warm and smooth against his palm. The ache started in his gut and spread lower, gnawed at him with increasing intensity.

"Guy." Her eyes closed on a sigh. "What are you doing to me?"

He heard the tension in her voice, a mixture of confusion and need, of anger and anticipation. He felt all those things, too.

Sounds drifted from the party above, a seductive Nat King Cole song, indistinguishable murmurs of conversations, a woman's laugh. And still, standing here in the trees by the lake, it seemed as if they were miles away from people.

"I won't do anything you don't want me to do, Holly." He rubbed his thumb lightly over her cheek. "Now ask me what I want to do to you, with you."

Her eyes opened slowly and she met his gaze. "What do you want to do with me?"

"Everything," he whispered as he leaned closer and brushed his lips lightly over hers. "I want you more than I've ever wanted any woman in my life. I want to make love with you."

Her hand trembled as she placed a palm on his

chest. He went still, afraid she'd him push away, afraid that she wouldn't. He waited, heart pounding in his chest, his mouth hovering a fraction of an inch from hers.

Then her fingers twisted in his shirt as she dragged his lips to hers.

Eight

Over the past few days, Holly had convinced herself that she'd completely blown that first kiss out of proportion with her overactive mind. She'd thought she'd simply imagined that her knees had gone weak and her toes had curled.

She'd thought wrong.

Senses reeling, she clung to him, met the urgent thrust of his tongue with her own. He tasted like wild blackberries, no doubt from Mabel Wistrom's home-made tarts on the dessert table. She felt dizzy and exhilarated at the same time.

Alive. Completely and utterly alive.

From the lake, she heard the mama duck softly talking to her babies, felt the cool breeze slide over her bare shoulders. The scent of pine and cedar was heady. Like a child's top out of control, the world spun around her.

When he dragged his lips from hers, she moaned in protest.

"Holly," he whispered raggedly. "We need to go back."

"Back?" She brought her lips to his neck and when she nipped, he sucked in a breath. "You mean inside?"

"Good grief, no. I meant to your place." He chuckled softly. "Back inside is the *last* place I should go right now."

When he pulled his lower body flush with hers, she understood completely what he meant.

His arms tightened around her again and he dropped his head to claim her one more time. She parted her lips for him and his mouth moved over her, insistent, teasing, sensuous. Every cell in her body vibrated with anticipation. To torment him, she slid her hips slowly up, then down again. But the torment was not all his, she quickly realized, and the burning need she'd felt only a moment ago now turned into a deep, hot throb.

He wrenched himself free, his breathing ragged and fast. "Woman, you do that one more time and I'm going to forget we're only twenty yards from about three hundred people."

Heavens! She'd nearly forgotten herself. And while the idea of making love in this stand of trees, with the sound of the water lapping softly at the shore and the breeze whispering in the pines tempted her, it was probably not a good idea.

She heard a sudden burst of laughter from the patio above and the sound resonated in the night air.

Definitely not a good idea.

"This way."

She took his hand, led him through the trees, then up several steep, narrow steps until they came out on the other side of the community center. Several people milled around the front of the building, and Guy quickly pulled Holly behind a hedge of bushes to avoid being seen. She slipped off her shoes, started to laugh at the absurdity of what they were doing, but when he dragged her against him and kissed her thoroughly, her laughter turned to a moan.

Then they were off and running with Guy in the lead this time, keeping to the shadows, weaving between bushes and trees and buildings. They were both laughing as they dashed up her stairs. One high heel slipped from her fingers and tumbled back down the steps.

"Leave it," he said simply when she started to turn, then opened the door and hauled her inside.

He had her in his arms and backed up against the wall in a heartbeat. His mouth swooped down and devoured.

Breathless, she wrapped her arms around him and hung on, met every hungry, hot kiss. She'd never been kissed with such need, with such desperation. Had never felt such intense pleasure in return. It frightened her a little, yet strangely, her fear only intensified that pleasure.

And then his hands started to move.

Down her sides, up again, then down. Long, slow

strokes that set her blood on fire. His hands slid to her ribs and the tips of his fingers brushed the undersides of her breasts. She shivered at the delicious caress of his palms on her belly. When he moved upward and cupped her breasts in his large hands, she moaned.

"Guy," she gasped when his mouth left hers to pay attention to her earlobe. "Are you sure that you—"

She lost her thought when his thumbs found her nipples and moved in tiny circles over the hardened peaks. White-hot pleasure streaked from that spot to the ache between her legs. Her head fell limply back against the door while his mouth and hands relentlessly worked magic on her.

"That I what?" he murmured.

His mouth, hot and insistent, moved to her neck. "Your ribs," she said, her voice thick with desire. "Are you all right?"

He chuckled softly. "Oh, yeah. I'm more than all right."

And then suddenly he swept her up in his arms, holding her tightly to him as he carried her to the bedroom, his strides long and sure. She knew that the distance they covered together was the longest trip she would ever make. And once that trip was made, there would be no turning back.

She felt a moment of panic. Not fear of making love, that felt as right, as necessary, as taking her next breath. But she knew instinctively that what she felt went further and deeper than the act of making love.

She knew she'd be giving him much more than her body. She'd be giving him her heart.

But when he stopped beside the bed, when he let her body slide down his as he lowered her to the floor, when he tilted her face up to his and asked softly, "Are you sure?" she knew the truth.

He already had her heart.

The heart she'd so carefully guarded, so tenaciously protected all these years, now belonged to Guy Blackwolf.

With a certainty that rose from her very soul, she nodded slowly. "I'm sure."

She slipped the thin straps of her dress off her shoulders, then let it slide down her body. Black silk pooled around her feet. His eyes darkened and narrowed at the sight of her bare breasts, but when he moved to touch her, she shook her head.

"Not yet," she said softly, then reached for the buttons on his shirt. She forced herself to concentrate on her task rather than the piercing steel-gray eyes that consumed her. Except for the sliver of black satin panties that stretched across her hips, she was naked. As each button slid free, it surprised Holly that her fingers held steady while her heart raced furiously and her senses reeled.

His chest rose and fell, his breathing deepened and grew heavy. Raw power and hard muscle rippled under her palms as she slid her hands inside his shirt and up his bared chest. A light sprinkling of dark hair tickled her fingers. When she leaned forward and pressed her lips to an L-shaped scar a few inches under his collarbone, he drew in a sharp breath.

"I need to touch you," he growled impatiently.

Her lips moved down his chest. Still she shook her head. "You'll distract me."

"I'll do more than that when I get my hands on you."

"I've been warned," she murmured.

"That's a promise, darlin'," he rasped, then swore when she parted her lips and lightly swept her tongue over the flat, tiny bead of male nipple. His words electrified her. She could feel the wild pounding of his heart under her hands and mouth; the explosive energy coiled tightly inside his strong body. All that magnificent power right under her fingertips, waiting to be released. The thought aroused her as much as frightened.

Who was this woman? she wondered as if she'd stepped outside herself and were watching instead of actively participating in this erotic display of intimacy. Certainly no woman she'd ever met before. The Holly Douglas she knew had never been a seductress or a femme fatale. She'd never wanted to be.

But she wanted to now. More than she'd ever dreamed possible.

A primitive, urgent need took hold of her. She raked her fingernails down his chest to his flat, hard stomach, took pleasure in the knowledge that his solidity didn't stop there.

While her fingers worked open his belt buckle, she lifted her gaze to his, saw the flames of desire behind his smoke-dark eyes. The fierce intensity of his gaze shot through her like a lightning bolt. She lowered his zipper slowly, the sound no more than a soft hiss, then spread her fingers over velvet steel as she slid upward again to the waistband of his black sports briefs.

All the while she kept her eyes steady with his, savoring not only the feel of him, but the look in his eyes that told her he wanted, that he needed her as much as she needed him. Her hands slid under snug stretch cotton, then felt hot, smooth skin as she slid them down again. Only then did her gaze lower.

Her breath caught.

Her gaze flew back to his. A wicked smile touched his mouth and his eyes glinted with a mix of amusement and desire.

Without touching her, he leaned close, toed off his shoes, then stepped out of his slacks as he lightly kissed the tip of her nose. "Don't move," he whispered.

And then, all sinew and rippling muscle, he was gone.

Don't move?

She was still holding her breath when he walked back in with a foil packet in his hand. Relieved, she slowly exhaled and allowed herself to fully enjoy the glorious sight of him. Long, powerful legs, broad shoulders, lean hips. He was obviously comfortable with his body, unconcerned that he was not only naked, but fully aroused. When he moved toward her with purpose and intent, her heart slammed against her ribs.

He set the packet on the nightstand, then turned to her.

The look he gave her nearly melted her on the spot.

If he hadn't reached for her then, if he hadn't pulled her into his arms, she was certain her knees would have given out.

She wound her arms around his neck, held on tight, and together they made the long journey to the bed.

"I thought about this," he murmured as he dragged his mouth over her jaw and down her neck. "I tried not to, but I couldn't get you out of my mind, wondering what you would taste like, what you would feel like."

Fire skittered over her skin at the touch of his teeth and mouth on her skin. "What do I feel like?" she asked breathlessly, wanting to know his every thought. "Tell me."

He rose on one elbow to keep his weight off her, lifted his face to gaze into her eyes. "Soft," he whispered, brought his lips to hers, nibbled on one corner. "Incredibly sweet." His hand moved down her throat, paused. "Like a mythical enchantress who's cast a spell over me."

She laughed at that, but his words made her feel special. And she desperately needed to feel special. Needed to know that she wouldn't be like every other woman he'd known before or would know in the future. She couldn't think about that now, didn't want to ever think about what it would be like when he was gone.

And when his hand slid lower, when his mouth moved to her breast, it was impossible to think at all. On a sigh, she closed her eyes and let every sensation, each one more intense than the one before, roll through her.

She never would have thought it possible to feel pleasure this intense, this powerful. His hands caressed, then cupped her breasts; his mouth closed over one nipple, lightly sucked as his hot, wet tongue lavished attention to the hardened tip. On a moan, she arched upward, dragged her hands through his thick hair and pulled him closer still.

Guy had wanted to be gentle, to move slowly with Holly, but her soft little moan and the innocent lift of her body urging him on was the end of his control. His hands tightened on her body and he drew her tightly into his mouth with an urgency that stunned him. She gasped at the sudden shift in mood, dug her own fingers tighter against his scalp.

"Guy," she pleaded. "Please…yes, oh, yes, do that…"

He turned his attention to her other breast, felt more than heard his own deep moan when her hands moved restlessly over his shoulders and back. The feel of her pebbled nipple against his tongue, the sound of her quick breaths, made his blood pound furiously in his temple.

His need for her made him rougher than he'd intended, but when he tried to pull back she made a whimpering sound and writhed under him and he was over the edge again. Impatient, he yanked the thin undergarment from her hips and with that small rip of satin, she was completely naked to him.

His hand moved to her belly, then lower to dip into the heat of her body, stroked her until she sobbed his name.

No more reason. No logic. No control. He simply had to have her.

He reached for the packet beside the nightstand, tore it open. A moment later, he took her face in his hands as he moved between her legs. She welcomed him, wrapped herself around him and drew him closer.

He slid inside.

It seemed that the world shifted and changed, that nothing and no one else existed outside this place. Their gazes met and held; he watched her eyes turn like fall leaves: from a glorious golden color to a deep, warm shade of amber. The intensity took his breath, made his pounding heart skip a beat. He'd never experienced anything like this in his life. He wasn't prepared for the emotion that gripped him and held on like the claw of some great winged beast.

But when she moved her hips, when she sighed his name, when she ran her hands down his chest to where they were joined, the need once again returned with a force that stole every other thought from him. He moved inside her, slowly at first, then faster, taking them both closer to the edge. Her body embraced his, met him stroke for stroke, matched the pulsing, erotic rhythm.

And when they reached the edge, when there was nowhere else to go, they held on tightly to each other and tumbled over together.

"I may never move again."

Holly laughed softly at Guy's hoarse whisper. She lay in the crook of his arm, one leg resting intimately over his, her head on his shoulder and her hand on his chest. She felt the heavy thud of his heart under her palm and knew that it matched her own.

Every nerve in her body still hummed with pleasure. If she were a cat, she'd be purring loud enough to make the walls shake. It amazed her, that she could feel so exhilarated, yet so completely relaxed at the same time.

She'd had only one intimate relationship before. In Texas, a man she'd dated a long time and felt comfortable with. But though she'd cared deeply for him, she'd never seen fireworks or heard bells ringing. Making love had never moved the earth or shattered her soul.

Until now.

This was a moment she'd have to hold onto, she knew. After he was gone, this would be all she would have.

She pushed those thoughts, and the pain they brought with them, aside. She was determined to enjoy what little time they did have. Three days. Less than seventy-two hours. She intended to make every minute count.

Slowly she stretched, rose on her elbow to gaze down at him. His eyes were closed and his breathing had steadied.

"Blackwolf, if you fall asleep, so help me, I'll pluck your chest hairs out one by one."

He opened one eye on a grimace. "So you're into torture, are you? I never would have thought it. Holly Douglas, Mistress of Pain and Earthly Delights. Has a nice ring to it."

"You're impossible." Shaking her head, she spread her fingers over his chest.

He lifted a finger to her cheek, then lightly traced a path across her jaw. "And you are incredible."

The simple touch of his fingertip made her tingle from head to toe. She wanted to believe him, believe that what had just happened between them was as special for him as it had been for her. But was she being naive? she wondered. Did she want so badly to believe it, that it clouded her thinking?

Perhaps ignorance was bliss, she thought. Maybe there were times it was better not to know the truth.

It would be easier for both of them to keep things simple and easy, she decided. Determined to do just that, she smiled and softly raked her fingernails over his chest. "Blackwolf," she murmured. "Such a nice Irish name."

"My father was Cherokee, my mother was from Naples. They met when he was in the Air Force and she was waiting tables in a nightclub. I don't remember much about her, except that she was beautiful and she used to yell at me, 'Guitano Antonio Blackwolf, you such a bad boy. I tell you papa when he comes home.'"

"Guitano Antonio, is it?" Holly smiled, slid her hand below his rib cage to his flat, solid stomach, then lower still. "And were you a bad boy?"

Suddenly she was on her back and he was grinning down at her with a wicked look in his eyes.

"Very bad," he murmured roughly and brought his mouth to hers.

His kiss was long and deep and surprisingly gentle.

She wrapped her arms around him and let herself go completely. As the fever built between them again, as it swept them away, she did something that she'd never allowed herself to do before.

She fell in love.

When Guy woke four hours later, the sheets and pillow beside him were as empty as they were cold. He sat, swiped at his face, gave his neck a twist to the left until he heard a crack, then swung his legs over the side of the bed.

The green display of the nightstand clock switched from 4:32 to 4:33. Way too early to be up, Guy thought. Not just because it was Sunday and Holly's store was closed, but because neither one of them had gotten much sleep last night. They'd been just a little bit busy.

He smiled, remembering in precise detail how they'd kept each other busy.

His smile faded. He was such an idiot. He'd had some foolish notion that once they'd made love the need that had been clawing at his insides would ease. If anything, now that he knew what her skin felt like under his hands, the way she came alive when he touched her, the way her soft lips parted and her eyes darkened when he slid inside her…

How could he know these things, remember all that, and not want her again and again?

But there was no place for him in her world, or for her in his. He flew in and flew out at a moment's notice, was gone most of the time, usually in remote areas. He wasn't a picket fence, nine-to-five kind of guy. He'd seen how she was with those kids at the school. She'd be a great mother. And he'd be a father who was never home. He knew what that was like for a kid. He'd been there, and it was a lousy place to be.

Sighing heavily, he slid out of bed and pulled on the slacks he'd worn last night that were still on the floor. He dragged his hands through his hair, then found her in the kitchen.

She stood at the window, her robe belted at her waist, staring out into the early morning. With her hair long and tousled around her shoulders, her skin flushed and her lips still rosy from his kisses, he thought she'd never looked more beautiful. He wanted to know what she was thinking, what she was feeling, but somehow, he didn't think he had the right to ask.

He waited a moment, until he could breathe again, then moved behind her. "Hey," he said softly.

"Hey, yourself."

Relief poured through him when she leaned back against him. Only now did he realize that he'd been afraid she would have turned away from him. Afraid that she would have regrets.

He wrapped his arms around her and they stood there in the early-morning silence, neither one of them speaking, a transition from the passion of the night before and the reality, the uncertainty, of a new day.

"I spoke to him once," she said softly. "In my whole life, just once."

Her voice had an empty, hollow tone to it. Guy

knew that the "him" she referred to was Cameron Fortune.

"I was only eight at the time." She continued to stare, unblinking, out the window. "My mother had been drinking and she called him, was pleading with him to talk to her, to come and meet me."

Guy wanted to stop her, to turn her in his arms, kiss her, make love to her again, anything to make her forget, if only for a moment, all the bad times. But he knew instinctively she needed to tell him. Not for him, but for herself.

"They were arguing," she went on after a moment. "When my mother started to cry I grabbed the phone and begged him to come be my daddy and take care of me and my mommy."

Outside, a pickup with fishing gear in the bed rumbled by. "That's Jim Turner and his son, Skip," she said absently. "They go out on the lake every Sunday morning before church."

Guy pressed his lips together, waited, then she turned slowly and stared at his chest. "Do you know what he said to me? He said, 'Tell your mother never to call my house again.' Then he hung up."

He swore hotly under his breath, pulled her into the circle of his arms and held her close. Guy wished to God that Cameron Fortune was alive just so he could have one good solid swing at the bastard.

"Maybe you're right," she said softly. "Maybe I am afraid to meet the Fortunes. Afraid they might reject me, too." Her eyes were bright when she looked up at him. "Maybe it is time to face that fear."

He tucked a strand of hair behind her ear, wanting nothing more than to take her back to bed. "What are you saying?"

"I'm saying—" her gaze held his "—that I'm going to Texas."

His hand stilled. "Are you sure?"

"I'm sure."

"All right then." He sighed. "I'm going with you."

"I'm a big girl, Blackwolf." The smile she gave him was crooked. "You don't need to go with me."

"Yeah," he said quietly. "I do need to."

She looked at him for a long moment, then nodded as she moved back into his arms. "Thank you."

This was what he'd come here for: to change her mind about meeting the Fortunes. The only reason he'd come. So why, now that she'd finally agreed, did he want to tell her not to go?

Damned if he knew.

Confused, he simply held her. And told himself that if even one member of that family hurt her, he'd deal with them himself.

Nine

The Texas Holly knew hadn't changed much in three years. The town of Gibson had a new, ten-store shopping center with a Box Office Hits Video and Williams Grocery Mart, but other than that, everything else looked pretty much the same. The gas station on Henley Avenue and Ford Street still had faded green siding; the red, white and blue barber pole still turned in front of Billy's Barber Shop and the Mustang Diner still had a large flashing neon sign in the shape of a horse.

As a child, Holly had always been fascinated by that sign. The legs flashed to simulate movement and the horse, with its mane flying in the wind, ran and ran and ran. Then one day, just four weeks after her mother had died, Holly stared at that sign and realized that for all its effort, the horse never went anywhere. It just stayed where it was, like a hamster on a wheel.

Two days later she'd packed everything she could fit into her car, quit her job at the drugstore and headed for Alaska and became an entrepreneur.

And now she was back, standing in front of the small white trailer that she'd been raised in. The new owners had done some upgrades: a fenced-in porch and new siding, plus a flower bed in front filled with bluebonnets and black-eyed Susans that didn't seem to mind the scorching afternoon sun.

"You okay?"

She turned at the sound of Guy's voice. He'd been waiting for her in the black Taurus they'd rented only an hour ago at the airport, but now he came up behind her and slipped his arms around her.

She smiled at him. "I'm fine."

It seemed like a lifetime had passed since yesterday when they'd flown out of Twin Pines with the insurance adjuster after he'd pronounced Guy's airplane a total loss. They'd spent the night in Seattle at Guy's apartment, caught an early-morning flight from Seattle to the airport in San Antonio, then driven to Holly's hometown where they'd checked into a room at The Gibson Motel.

Tomorrow she would meet with Ryan and Miranda, but tonight she'd wanted to be here, in the town where she'd been raised, where she could be close to what was familiar to her.

Where she could be close to Guy.

She knew her time with him was temporary, but she refused to let that undermine the pleasure she felt when they were together. Only later, after she flew back to Twin Pines and he went home to Seattle, would she allow herself to think about and then deal with the inevitable pain. For now, she wanted only to remember these moments of sharing, of togetherness. The moments of intimacy, of being loved and feeling loved. She would cherish each precious moment.

So for now, she would think only of the present. And that's what it was, she realized. A present.

Smiling, she leaned back against him, then pointed to a thickly wooded area about a hundred yards from the trailer. "There's a creek and fishing hole behind those oaks and boulders over there. When I was twelve, I used to go swimming in there with Timmy John and Billy Ray."

"Timmy John and Billy Ray?"

She chuckled at the you've-got-to-be-kidding tone in his voice. "The Thompson brothers. They lived three trailers down from mine. They were twelve and thirteen and the only other kids in the park close to my age at that time. For the year that they lived here, they let me tag along with them sometimes."

"Yeah?" He raised a brow. "They do anything I have to find them and beat them up for?"

"They were perfect gentlemen." She gave a delicate sniff. "In fact, Billy Ray swore in front of me one time and Timmy John gave him a black eye and made him apologize. I fell madly in love with T.J. after that and followed him around for the next two months. Then they moved and I never saw either of them again."

"Good." His arms closed tighter around her. "I

can't picture you still living here with someone named Timmy John and a pack of Timmy John Jr's. tugging on the hem of your cotton housecoat.''

"Is that so?'' She glanced over her shoulder at him. "And just how *do* you picture me?''

"Wearing black silk,'' he said and nibbled at her ear. "Stretched out on white satin sheets, with diamonds at your throat and perfume that costs a thousand dollars an ounce.''

She knew he was teasing, but his words seduced her as much as his lips on her ear. Since the night they'd made love, there had been no question that he wanted her or that she had wanted him right back. No games, no pretending, no guile. They made love with an openness, an honesty, and an intensity she wouldn't have thought existed.

She would cherish every moment with him, she told herself. No regrets.

When his lips grazed her neck, she shivered. "Thousand dollar an ounce perfume? Where would I find that?''

"In Paris,'' he murmured. "You'd fly in on your private jet for breakfast in Versailles, then shop in the afternoon.''

"And at night?'' Her eyes drifted closed when his mouth slid back up to her ear. "What would I do at night?''

"Well,'' he whispered, "you'd have to be back home in time to make dinner for your husband and eight kids, of course. A man's gotta eat, ya know.''

"Good try, Blackwolf.'' Laughing, she leaned back against him, letting herself enjoy the moment. "But

I don't cook, remember? You sure you aren't fantasizing about Marcy Pruitt on those satin sheets?''

"Nope." He turned her to face him, brushed his lips with hers. "Come back to the motel with me, Holly, and I'll show you exactly who and what I've been fantasizing about."

Smiling, she touched his cheek with her fingertips. "Okay."

When Guy slipped the key into the motel room lock, he heard the sound of the phone ringing from inside. He looked at Holly, watched the smile that had been on her lips fade as she stared at the phone. "You want me to answer it?" he asked.

She shook her head, then walked to the phone on the nightstand beside the king-size bed. She hesitated between rings, drew in a deep breath, then picked the receiver up.

"Hello?"

She glanced at him, and Guy's gut tightened at the flash of fear in her eyes. When she turned her back to him, he clenched his jaw and shoved his hands into his pockets to keep himself from reaching for her. He knew that she would want to do this herself, that she needed to do this herself.

"Yes, that would be fine," she said into the phone, then picked up the motel pen on the nightstand and wrote something on the notepad sitting there. "All right. I'll see you then."

She hung up the phone quietly, stared at it for a long moment.

"Is everything all right?" Guy asked.

"That was Miranda. My—" She hesitated. "My father's sister. She said that Ryan is still in the hospital and that he's doing much better, but the doctors want to observe him a few more days. She asked if it would be all right if I met with her at the ranch tomorrow at two-thirty. She has some business matters to handle for Ryan."

She turned then, reached for her suitcase that sat on the valet stand beside the bed. "I got directions," she went on. Her voice was strained. "I wasn't sure if you'd ever been to the ranch. I hear it's really something."

Guy watched her zip her suitcase open and busy herself with the contents inside, moving things around while she rambled. "Or if you'd prefer to stay here, I can take the car and be back in time for dinner. Or I could drop you off somewhere and you could—"

"Holly." He closed the distance between them, took hold of her shoulders and turned her to face him.

"What?" Her eyes were wide and innocent, but in spite of her light chatter and easy tone, he saw the edge of apprehension.

"It's okay to be a little nervous," he told her.

"Don't be silly." She laughed dryly. "I'm not nervous."

"You're trembling."

"Am I?"

"Yes, you are. Come sit down."

She shook her head. "I can't sit down."

"And why is that?"

"Because I think I'm going to throw up."

Chuckling, he tugged her stiff body into his arms.

"Just take a deep breath," he said and eased her down to sit on the side of the bed.

She gulped in some air, then slowly released it.

"Better?"

She nodded slowly. "You must think I'm a big baby."

"No, I don't think you're a baby." He combed his fingers through her hair. "I think you're probably the bravest woman I've ever met."

"Right." She rolled her eyes. "That's why it feels like there's a blender inside my stomach."

"The fact that you're afraid doesn't make you a coward," he said gently. "But refusing to face that fear would. Like Zachary."

"Zachary?"

"Zachary Zebra." He smiled at the surprise on her face. "The story you read to the kids the day I was taking a walk and just happened by."

"Just happened by?" She lifted one brow. "Right."

"Anyway—" he took her hands in his; her fingers were like ice "—you were terrific."

"It's the kids that are terrific." Her cheeks flushed at his compliment.

I adore you, he almost said, but caught himself. The words would have been easy to say if he was teasing or flirting. But the fact that he truly meant them, that his chest ached with a feeling so unfamiliar to him, made him hold back. Startled him.

And yet, for that moment, it made him wonder, too...

Later, he told himself. He'd think about all this

later. Right now he simply wanted to hold her, to warm her chilled hands and erase the worry in her eyes.

When he tugged her gently into his arms, she rested her cheek on his shoulder. "She didn't sound like a horrible person," she said quietly.

"Miranda?"

She nodded. "I always thought of them, all the Fortunes, that way. Guilt by association."

"You had a right to be angry." She'd stopped trembling, he noted. He brought her hand to his mouth, kissed each knuckle in turn and felt the warmth return to her fingers.

"At Cameron Fortune, yes." She sighed, relaxed her stiff shoulders. "But to assume anyone and everyone connected to him was bad, was hardly reasonable. When I went to Alaska, I'd somehow convinced myself that my life in Texas never existed. That every snide remark that had ever been made to me, every sideways glance, every pitiful look, would simply disappear from my memory. When that first letter came, I was so furious they'd contacted me in Alaska, I burned it. There were three more after that, I sent them all back unopened. I thought they would give up and leave me alone. I *wanted* them to leave me alone."

She pulled away from him, touched his cheek as she gazed into his eyes. "And then you showed up. A bit dramatically, I might add."

"Got your attention, didn't I?" he teased, pressed his lips into the palm of her hand.

"Oh, yeah." She smiled, watched him through

heavy-lidded eyes as he moved his mouth to her wrist. "But you know what I really noticed about you that first day?"

"My charming personality?" He nibbled on the tender flesh under his lips, felt her pulse speed up. "My extraordinary sense of humor? The manly way I sank after my plane crashed?"

Her laugh was thick and seductive as he worked his way up to her elbow. "Your feet."

His feet? He lifted his head and frowned at her. "You noticed my feet?"

"Uh-huh," she murmured. "When you were in Doc's office, sitting on the table. I thought your bare feet were sexy." Her eyes drifted closed. "Could you please keep doing what you were doing just now?"

"What? Oh." He turned his attention back to the inside of her elbow. "Well, shoot, if I'd have known you had a thing for feet, I would have kept my shoes and socks off and walked around on my hands."

"I didn't say I had a *thing* for feet." She sighed with pleasure when he tasted the rapid pulse in the crook of her arm. "I just happened to notice yours."

"What else did you notice?" he asked as his mouth slid over her warm skin.

"Well, let's see." Her voice turned smoky. "I think you have good posture."

"Thanks." He knew she was teasing now and he smiled against the soft, smooth skin of her inner arm. "Anything else?"

"Ears," she said breathlessly, and when his mouth moved to her breast, her fingers raked through his thick hair. "You have sexy ears."

"So you like my legs, my posture and my ears." He lightly cupped her breasts while he nuzzled through the thin cotton of her tank top. "I bet you say that to all the boys."

"Just the ones I want to get in bed." She gasped softly when he slid his hands under her top. "So is it working?"

In one fluid movement, he drew her top up and over her head. "Oh, yeah," he murmured and eased her back on the bed. "It's working just fine."

How wonderful it felt to be swept away like this, Holly thought. To simply close her eyes and let herself float on a sea of sensuality where nothing and no one existed but the two of them. His hands slid over her body, his mouth moved tenderly, teasing, tasting, and each touch was like a tiny wave that lapped gently at her skin, again and again, soothing even as it excited.

"So what—" she arched upward when he palmed her breasts in his large, rough hands "—did you first notice about me?"

"Your eyes," he whispered against her neck, his voice raw. "They made me think of wild honey."

She smiled at that, tilted her head to allow his mouth to move more freely. He accepted the invitation, blazed kisses upward to her jaw, her chin, then found her mouth and brushed his lips over hers.

"I've wanted you from that first moment," he said softly, teased the corner of her mouth with his lips while he rubbed her pebbled nipples with his thumbs. "Keeping my hands off you nearly drove me crazy."

Pleasure rushed through her veins, throbbed in her

breasts and between her legs. She squirmed under him, wrapped her arms around his neck and drew him closer. "You're driving me crazy now, Blackwolf. Make love to me. Please."

"I am, sweetheart, I am."

He kissed her, not hard like she wanted him to, but gently, tenderly, and the sweetness of it nearly made her weep with the love she felt for him. On a moan, she clung to him, wanting this moment to be endless. This man owned her, she thought almost with despair. He owned her heart, her body, her soul. She gave herself willingly to him, completely.

She whispered his name, pleaded with him to hurry, but still he took his time, a long, sensual exploration of her body that left her weak and exhilarated at the same time. Slow, lingering kisses, and soft, lazy caresses. She felt the beat of his heart, heavy and hard, heard the pulsing in her own head.

Clothes fell away until they were skin to skin, soaking in the heat of each other. His arms were muscled, like steel against hers, his legs long and powerful and beautifully naked. She wrapped herself around that strength, felt an urgency, a desperation unlike anything she'd ever known before.

Need drove her, passion guided her, love empowered her. She rose up to him, brought him inside her, intensifying the pleasure until she thought she might not be able to bear it one moment longer. She dragged her hands through his hair when he bent over her, raked her fingernails over his shoulders while his teeth and lips worked miracles on her breasts. His tongue teased one hardened nipple, then he pulled her hard into his mouth and she cried out his name.

Desire. It engulfed them, seeped into every pore, every cell. She could taste it on his lips, feel it on his skin, hear it in his sharp, ragged breaths. Desire. Wild and wonderful, it washed over them, through them. She slid her hands down his strong back to the taut muscles of his rear, felt the coiled heat and gloried in it. For this moment, she knew that he was hers as much as she was his. She would have laughed at the joy she felt from that knowledge, but his lips found hers again and once again she was swept away.

This time, there was nothing gentle in his kiss. It was a kiss meant to ravage, to consume. She met him, felt the same hot, crazed need as he did. She heard her heart pounding in her head...no, not one heart, she thought. Two hearts...

Gasping, Guy dragged his mouth from hers.

"Holly." His voice was rough and hoarse.

She responded by wrapping her arms around his neck and dragging his mouth back to hers. Her lips were swollen and moist and unable to help himself, Guy slid back into the sweetness and lost himself. He couldn't get enough of her, he thought. It didn't matter how much she gave or how much he took, it still just wasn't enough.

Once again, he pulled away. "Holly. Look at me."

"Hmm?"

She was already reaching for him, but he took her hands, linked them with his and raised them over her head. "Look at me," he repeated, struggled for breath as he looked down at her.

She opened her eyes slowly, gazed up at him through a heavy haze of passion.

"You're the most beautiful, special woman I've ever known."

She smiled at that, eased her body upward, offering herself to him. Blood surged through his veins, hot and pulsing, but he wanted her to know, wanted her to understand.

"I mean it," he said more gently. "There's never been anyone like you before." And the thought that there never would again slammed into his gut, intensified the urgency already pounding in his body.

"Thank you," she murmured, and because she was unable to touch him with her hands, she used her eyes, let her gaze slide hotly over his body to where they were joined, then moved her hips.

He moaned, but still held onto her hands. The sight of her long, slender, glorious body stretched out under him, eyes half-closed and glazed with need, the heavy rise and fall of her beautiful, full breasts. He bent and kissed the rosy tip of each pearled nipple, heard the soft moan slide from Holly's lips, then the whimper when he took first one nipple into his mouth and tasted, then moved to the other.

She cried out his name as she arched upward, taut as the string of a bow, ready to be plucked. But still he held her hands firmly in his, wanting, needing to know that she was his completely.

"Now, please now," she whispered. "I need you."

Nothing could have ever aroused him more than those words from her. Something inside him snapped and he knew he couldn't wait one moment longer.

"Yes." He moved inside her. "Now."

Velvet-steel against soft silk. Wolf eyes locked to golden-honey eyes. The rhythm built, sensations spiraled, increased. A reckless, wild need that drove them to that sharp, jagged edge where they both tumbled over.

Holly lay in his arms, unable to move for what felt like a lifetime. She was still floating, and in her mind, she watched each soft, billowy cloud drift slowly by. How clear the sky was up here, she thought. The air fresh and clean. She felt renewed, reborn.

"You okay?" she heard him ask from behind one of her clouds and all she could do was nod and sigh.

The sound of his soft chuckle made her smile, as well.

The tip of his finger traced a slow path down her neck, and the featherlight touch sent waves of warm ripples over her skin. She snuggled closer into the crook of his arm, breathed in the mingled scent of man and woman. A fine sheen of perspiration cooled their bodies. She shivered when his fingertip skimmed the rise of her breast.

"Holly."

With tremendous effort, she opened her eyes and looked at him. His hair was rumpled, his eyes a deep, dark gray.

"I really hadn't intended that to happen."

She lifted her head, arched a brow. "Oh?"

"I mean, before, after you got that phone call from Miranda. You were nervous and upset. I just wanted to take your mind away from that."

"You succeeded." She placed her hands on his chest and rested her chin on top, then smiled at him. "And very well, I might add."

"Yeah?" He gave her a sideways grin.

"Yeah." She reached out and gently touched the scar on his temple. It seemed like years ago that he'd fallen out of the sky and landed in her life. She wondered if after he was gone, if he would think of her when he looked at that scar.

Her scars, she thought, would be in her heart.

He took her fingers in his hand and brought them to his mouth, then nibbled on her. "You taste good," he murmured.

"I know a terrific BBQ place in town if you're hungry." She felt her pulse jump with each tiny bite of his teeth on her fingertips. "They have ribs so tender they melt in your mouth."

She gasped as he rolled her onto her back.

"Ribs that melt in your mouth?" He traced each one of her ribs with his fingertips, then slid upward, cupped her breasts in his palms. "Sounds good."

"Are you trying to distract me again?" she asked, struggling to breathe as his hands kneaded her soft flesh.

"Yeah." He bent down, kissed her belly, her hip, moved to the vee of her thighs. "Is it working?"

"Oh, yes." She sucked in a breath as his mouth moved over her. *"Oh, yes…"*

Ten

The Double Crown Ranch was everything Holly had ever imagined and more: Cattle grazing on land farther than the eye could see, quarter horses gathered under the shade of an old, beautiful oak, fences that seemed to stretch forever. It was a scene from a postcard or a book on beautiful Texas landscapes.

And it was the home of Ryan Fortune.

She felt like a child sitting in the passenger's seat of the car, wanting to press her nose to the window and take in every magnificent detail. It was all she could do not to constantly yell, "Wow, look at that!" If her palms weren't sweating and her insides weren't shaking so fiercely, she just might have. She should have worn the red-print sundress she'd packed instead of the pale yellow sleeveless T-shirt and khaki slacks, she told herself. She didn't fit in here, amongst all

this grandeur. She didn't belong here. Desperately she
wanted to tell Guy to turn the car around right now
and go back.

No. She pressed her lips firmly together.

No going back. Not now. Not after coming all this
way. She'd see this through, no matter what.

"If you don't breathe," Guy said from the other
side of the car, "you're going to pass out."

She *had* been holding her breath, she realized and
glanced over at him with a sheepish look. She didn't
think she could have done this without him. She knew
that she wouldn't have wanted to.

Two weeks ago, if anyone had told her that she'd
be head over heels in love with a man who was only
passing through her life, a man who would never love
her back, and that man would be escorting her to
Texas to meet Cameron Fortune's family, she would
have split a gut laughing.

Two weeks was a very long time.

A lifetime, she thought and took her eyes off the
landscape for a moment to look at Guy. Dressed in
jeans, a black polo shirt and cowboy boots, he looked
as handsome as he did relaxed behind the wheel. He
was a man who was as comfortable with himself as
he was with other people. A man who made her laugh
with one breath, then thrilled her with the next. A
man who made her want more than she'd ever wanted
before.

He'd made love to her yesterday and last night with
such tenderness, then such passion, she'd let herself
wonder, just for a moment, if it were possible. That
somehow, just maybe, he could love her back. That

he might want more than a few days or a few weeks with her. That he might want something…permanent.

Dangerous thinking, she knew. Stupid thinking. Love did that to a person. Made them do foolish things, think foolish things.

Holly refused to be a fool for any man, no matter how much she loved him. Her mother had done that, and where had it gotten her? She'd been a heartbroken, shattered woman who'd wasted her life on a man who didn't love her back. And while Holly certainly didn't compare Guy to Cameron Fortune, she knew in her heart that if she let him, he had that kind of power over her, the kind of power that could destroy.

She couldn't allow that. She *refused* to waste her life. She wouldn't cry when he went back to Seattle and she went back to Alaska. She folded her hands tightly in her lap and straightened her shoulders. She *wouldn't* cry.

What she *would* do, she told herself, is enjoy each and every minute with him, remember every touch, every look, every beautiful moment they'd shared. She'd remember and she'd smile with fondness and affection.

And love.

To prove that she could do just that, she forced herself to concentrate on *this* moment, *this* memory, of riding in the car with him and seeing Ryan Fortune's ranch for the first time.

"This is all so incredible," she said, turning back to look through the window. "So…big. Oh my heavens, there's the house!"

To say that the house was enormous was an understatement. The style was that of a Spanish hacienda. She could also see the barn not far from the house and what looked like several corrals. Other structures, smaller and quite a distance from the main house, appeared to be additional living quarters, probably for the hired help, Holly decided.

This was where Cameron Fortune had been born. Where he was raised as a child and lived as an adult. Not more than an hour from where Holly and her mother lived, and he hadn't come to see either one of them even once. The anger she'd once felt turned to simple sadness. She could only feel sorry for the man who'd been given so much, yet done so little with his life.

"Ready?"

She'd been so lost in thought she hadn't realized they were already parked in front of the house and he'd shut off the engine. She glanced at Guy and nodded stiffly. "Ready."

A moment later, with Guy beside her, she stared at the enormous front door.

"You want me to knock?" he asked.

She shook her head, then sucked in a breath and rapped three times. A pretty blonde wearing a white cotton blouse and black slacks opened the door. She was probably in her late forties, with blue eyes and a lovely smile.

"Holly." The woman's face lit up as she reached out and grasped one of Holly's hands in both of her own. "I'm your Aunt Miranda. Your Uncle Ryan and I are so happy you're here."

"Thank you." *Aunt Miranda. Uncle Ryan.* How

strange that sounded to Holly. And yet, at the same time, it made her chest tighten with longing. Miranda's grip was firm and warm and the knot in Holly's stomach loosened a notch.

"And you must be Guy," Miranda said before Holly could introduce him. "Thank you so much for bringing my niece here. Flynn spoke very highly of you. Now please, both of you, come in before you melt out here in this heat."

Guy's hand on the small of her back calmed Holly's nerves. She glanced at him as they followed Miranda through the entry. He winked at her, then smiled. She smiled back, grateful that he was with her.

Miranda led them into a large living room. The ceilings were high-beamed, the decor traditional, with brown leather couches and a massive stone fireplace. Spanish blankets, prints and paintings adorned the walls. On a side table, a crystal vase filled with yellow roses lightly scented the air.

"Please sit." Miranda gestured to a couch with Navajo print pillows, then sat down next to Holly. A petite Hispanic maid brought out a tray with a pitcher of iced tea, set it on the coffee table in front of the couch, then quietly left. "Your Aunt Lily is at the hospital, but you'll meet her later."

Aunt Lily. That was Ryan's wife, Holly remembered. To keep her hands busy, Holly accepted a glass of iced tea, but Guy declined.

"How is…Uncle Ryan?" Holly asked while Miranda poured the tea. She couldn't have imagined she'd ever refer to Ryan Fortune as her uncle, but now, after meeting Miranda, after hearing the woman actually refer to her as her niece, it wasn't nearly as difficult as Holly had thought it would be.

"He's going to be fine." With a smile, Miranda handed Holly her tea, but the smile never reached the woman's eyes. "He should be out of the hospital soon."

Something in Miranda's voice suggested there was more to Ryan's illness than she was saying. Holly's first reaction was not to pry, but she hadn't come all this way to be treated like an outsider. Either they accepted her now and trusted her, or she'd take the next plane back to Alaska and be done with the Fortune family forever.

Holly leveled her gaze at Miranda. "May I ask what was wrong?"

Miranda hesitated, glanced thoughtfully from Holly to Guy. Outside, in the distance somewhere, a dog barked.

"Anything you say to me," Holly said, "you can say to Guy, as well."

Miranda nodded, then seemed to make a decision. "The doctors are still running tests, but they have strong reason to believe that Ryan was poisoned."

"Poisoned?" Holly straightened, furrowed her brow. "But why? Who?"

With a sigh, Miranda shook her head. "We don't know. Ryan is an important, wealthy man. It's possible one of his business rivals or opponents might have done it for any number or reasons. The San Antonio police department has been called in."

Holly's hand tightened on her glass. "The police?"

"I'm afraid so. Detective Freddie Suarez will be handling the investigation." Miranda's eyes began to tear. "I'm so sorry that when you finally decided to come here, that this had to happen. Please don't let this frighten you away."

"I won't be frightened away," Holly said softly. She set her tea down, then reached out and covered Miranda's hand.

"Oh, Holly." Miranda glanced down at Holly's hand on hers, then looked back up into her eyes. "It's taken a long time to bring this family together. It means so much to your Uncle Ryan and myself, and everyone else, that you changed your mind and came to meet us. After what Cameron did to you and your mother, I realize how difficult it must be for you to come here. My brother was such a fool."

Miranda's voice quivered with emotion. She closed her eyes and sighed. "Not that I haven't done some foolish things myself. I only pray that it's not too late to make things right."

Holly had the distinct feeling that "making things right" involved more than inviting her brother's illegitimate daughter into the family. It was obvious that Miranda was dealing with demons of her own. Something was troubling the woman, Holly realized. Something deeply personal, as well as painful.

"You didn't do anything to me," Holly said gently. "And what Cameron did is in the past. What matters is now."

Miranda opened her eyes and nodded, then smiled. "Will you come to the hospital with me to visit your uncle? He's so anxious to finally meet you."

"Of course I'll come." It was all happening so fast. Holly's stomach did a flip. Would Ryan be as warm and welcoming as Miranda? What if he didn't like her? Once again, the urge to get in the car, drive straight to the airport and fly back home overwhelmed her.

Stop that, she told herself. So what if he didn't like her? She'd survive. She refused to turn tail and run. "We still need to check into the hotel in San Antonio. Why don't we meet you at the hospital?"

"Hotel!" Miranda shook her head. "But you're staying here, of course."

Holly started to protest, but Miranda held up a hand. "Lily would never forgive me if you didn't stay here. This house is huge. And besides, the rest of the family is coming over for dinner. Everyone's looking forward to meeting you."

Holly had no idea who "everyone" was, but her stomach went from flips to somersaults. She glanced at Guy, who nodded back. "Well, all right, then. Thank you."

"I'm sorry, Miss Miranda." The maid came back into the room. "Detective Suarez is calling for you. You can take it in Mr. Ryan's office if you like."

"Excuse me for a moment, please." The worry in Miranda's eyes that Holly had seen earlier was back now. "Louisa can show you to your rooms while I take this call, then we can drive to the hospital together."

Rooms? Holly felt her heart sink. Considering how little time she and Guy had left together, she didn't want to give up even one night with him. But it would be awkward at this point to explain their relationship, Holly realized. Not that she knew exactly what their relationship was.

Still, she glanced at Guy, hoped he would say something, put his arm around her and tell Miranda that they would only be needing one room. But he didn't. He simply nodded at Miranda and thanked her.

Was he already stepping back from her? she wondered. Or was he simply afraid that he might cause her embarrassment if they slept in the same room together?

After Miranda left, the maid led the way down a long hallway to their rooms, which were across from each other.

Close enough, she thought with a smile. When Guy went back outside to get their bags, she decided that she'd be paying him a midnight visit.

Her smile widened at the anticipation of slipping into his arms once again and making love with him. She glanced at her wristwatch and began to count the hours.

"Other than that scar on your forehead, you're looking pretty good for a man who crashed a plane in a lake."

Guy accepted the bottle of beer Flynn had brought him out on Ryan Fortune's patio. Inside the house, the "rest of the family" that Miranda had mentioned earlier were celebrating Holly's arrival. All the hugging and kissing and the open, genuine affection for each other truly amazed, as well as baffled him. Though he'd been introduced to everyone, and they'd all been friendly to him, Guy preferred to watch the festivities through one of the many French doors separating the living area from the outside patio.

"Nice to see you, too, Flynn," Guy said with a grin and meant it. Flynn had showed up an hour ago for the get-together with his new wife, Emma, who was, at the moment, feeding their newborn in one of the bedrooms. "And for your information, women like scars."

Flynn grinned back at him, then looked through the patio doors to where Holly was laughing with her cousin Kane and his wife, Allison. "Well, it's obvious at least one woman does. You wanna tell me what's going on with you two?"

"There's nothing going on." Guy took a sip from his bottle, watched as a pretty redhead whose name he couldn't remember came up to Holly and gave her a hug. He knew that Holly had agonized over what to wear this evening and had finally settled on black slacks, a pretty pink silk sleeveless blouse and a string of pearls. She looked beautiful, he thought, but then, she could have worn burlap and she'd still be gorgeous.

Flynn followed the direction of Guy's attention and raised one brow. "This is Flynn you're talking to, B.W. You want to try that again?"

"Give it a rest, Dog-Man," Guy said smoothly. "That P.I. nose of yours is working overtime."

"Just my eyes, pal. I'd have to be blind not to see the looks the two of you have been giving each other. If you aren't already sleeping together, you both sure as hell are thinking damn hard about it."

Dammit, anyway. All evening, Guy had been careful to keep his distance from Holly. She had enough to deal with meeting her family. What she didn't need was anyone questioning her relationship with a bush pilot from Seattle. But he should have known that he wouldn't be able to fool Flynn. They'd been through too much together, knew each other too well, for either one of them to pull one over on the other.

Guy shook his head as he stared at the beer in his hand. "It wouldn't work, Flynn. You know me. I spend more time in the air than on the ground. Holly deserves better than that."

"Seems to me she should be the one to make that decision," Flynn said. "Have you talked to her about it?"

Guy shook his head. "She's got her family now, a business of her own in Twin Pines. I can't give her what she wants, what she needs."

"Which is?"

He shrugged, couldn't help but drag his attention back to Holly. The smile on her face, the flush on her cheeks as she laughed with everyone around her, made his chest ache. When she'd come home from the hospital earlier after meeting her uncle, her eyes sparkling with excitement, it was all he could do to keep his hands off her. It was all he could do to keep his hands off her right now.

"She wants what all women want," Guy said evenly. "A wedding ring, kids, stability. Just thinking about all that makes me break into a cold sweat." Flynn grinned at him. "Yeah, well, that's what we all say before we take the plunge, buddy. You sure it's not the money that's scaring you off? It's not every day a guy marries a girl worth ten million dollars.''

Guy froze.

Ten million dollars?

He must have heard wrong. Slowly, very slowly, he turned his head and stared at Flynn. *"What* did you say?''

Flynn frowned, then cursed softly. "Guy, I'm sorry. I thought you knew. Obviously they haven't told Holly yet. She's about to inherit ten million dollars.''

Ten million dollars.

Guy felt his heart stop. He had certainly figured there would be some kind of money one day down the road, but ten million? If he'd wanted to, he couldn't have put two words together. He simply continued to stare at Flynn.

"It takes some getting used to," Flynn said with a grin. "Believe me, I know.''

"You mean, you—'' Guy struggled to breathe "—I mean, Emma. Her, too?''

Flynn nodded. "All the heirs, Guy.''

At that moment, Kane Fortune stuck his head out the door. "Hey, Flynn, Allison wants to take a family picture and I'm in charge of rounding up the herd.''

"Be right there.'' Flynn looked back at Guy and sighed heavily. "Look, Guy, I'm sorry I told you. Obviously Miranda and Ryan haven't told her yet, but it's no secret. Holly is about to become an extremely wealthy woman.''

Ten million dollars. Good Lord. Guy's hand tightened around the bottle in his hand. To say "extremely wealthy'' was one hell of an understatement. ''I'm happy for her,'' he finally managed to say. ''She's a great gal.''

''Great gal?'' Flynn laughed as he shook his head. ''Oh man, you do have it bad.''

''I don't have anything bad.'' Guy scowled at Flynn. ''Maybe I'm a little off balance here, that's all.''

''A little?'' Chuckling, Flynn slapped Guy on the back. ''Right. Keep telling yourself that, pal.''

''Ah, hah. Found you.''

Both men turned at the sound of Holly's voice from the French doors on the other side of the patio. Smiling brightly, she moved toward them, her gaze solely on Guy.

''I wondered where you'd been hiding all night. I should have known that you—'' She hesitated when both Guy and Flynn stared at her. Her smile dipped slightly, then she stopped and started to back away. ''I'm sorry, I didn't mean to intrude.''

''Of course you're not intruding,'' Flynn said smoothly. ''I'll take a beautiful woman's company over this ugly mug any day.''

Holly hesitated, glanced from Flynn to Guy. The smile she forced didn't quite reach her eyes. ''I'm supposed to drag you two in for pictures.''

''On my way.'' Flynn raised his bottle to Guy. ''See you inside, buddy.''

It didn't take a genius to see that the two men had been in a serious discussion, Holly thought as she watched Flynn go back into the house. And based on the way Guy was looking at her, it was easy to guess that the subject of their conversation was herself.

The fact that the evening was hot didn't seem to matter. Holly suddenly felt a chill shiver up her spine.

"I'm sorry if I interrupted." She carefully held her smile in place. "I'm sure you and Flynn have a lot to catch up on."

"We were caught up before dinner. Besides—" he nodded toward the French doors where inside, Flynn had joined Emma "—the only thing on his mind these days is that new wife and baby of his."

Flynn's wife, Emma, had been introduced to Holly as her cousin. There were more cousins, plus half sisters and half brothers she hadn't met yet, and her mind reeled just trying to keep everyone straight.

Since meeting her uncle Ryan at the hospital, the entire day had been a whirlwind. Her Aunt Miranda had been wonderful, and everyone she'd met so far had welcomed her with open arms. They were all warm, loving, accepting people. Every fear she'd had about meeting this family had completely dissipated.

She only had one fear now. A fear that twisted her stomach into knots and made her chest tighten until she could barely breathe.

It didn't take a genius to read the look in his eyes or the firm set of his jaw. He'd kept his distance from her all evening, carefully avoided her. And the way he'd stiffened when she'd walked out onto the patio just now only confirmed her fear: He was leaving.

He had done his duty, hadn't he? Brought her here to meet her family? What reason would he have to stick around?

None at all.

She wouldn't panic. She wouldn't run. She wouldn't put it off. To wait would only make it worse. Whatever it was, she'd deal with it right now. Right here.

"You weren't talking about Flynn's wife and baby just now, were you, Guy?" She leveled her gaze with his. "You were talking about me."

She saw the truth in his eyes. She'd been holding onto a tiny shred of hope, but the split second he looked away, she saw it and she knew. The chill she'd felt only a moment before now turned to cold dread.

"Holly, I should have told you before," he began, then looked away from her. "I'm sorry I didn't...you were busy with—"

"Just say it," she said tightly.

He pressed his lips together in a thin line. "I've got to get back to Seattle. I got a call today from Pelican. I've been offered a two-week position to fill in for another pilot and use one of their planes. I have to leave in an hour to catch the red-eye."

An hour? He was leaving in an hour, and this was the first she'd heard about it? The cold she felt turned to numbness. "I see."

He'd never promised her anything. No rings, no picket fences, certainly no happily-ever-happy. She had told herself she would settle for whatever time they'd spent together and be grateful for it, but the pathetic fact was she didn't want to settle and she wasn't grateful. In her heart, in her soul, she now knew that she'd been fooling herself. She wanted it all. She wanted him. Not just for a few days or a few weeks. Dammit, she'd wanted forever.

"Holly," he said gently. "I thought it would be easier to just say goodbye now. You're with your family, that's why you came. You don't need me."

Didn't need him? How could she possibly respond to that? She had to swallow back the scream that threatened to burst forth. Maybe she didn't need him. No more than air to breathe, she supposed. Or sleep. Or food.

But he wanted to let her down easy, she could see that. The gentle tone of his voice, the pain in his eyes. He cared for her, she was certain of that much. But not enough. Not nearly enough.

At this moment, she thought she hated him as much as she loved him.

She made herself smile. Not too wide; that would certainly be obvious. Not too little; that would look pitiful. Just an easy, soft smile that she might give him if he'd simply said hello or touched her arm.

"Relax, Blackwolf," she said smoothly. "I'm not going to fall apart on you, if that's what has you looking like you just stepped on a nail. Can I give you a lift to the airport?"

His lips pressed tightly together, and for one foolish moment, she thought maybe, that just maybe, he might reach for her. That he might tell her he couldn't go. Not without her.

But that moment slid like sand through her fingers and he shook his head. "Thanks, but the guest of honor can't very well just pick up and leave her own party. Flynn's got it covered. I'll call you when I get back to Seattle.''

That was a lie. They both knew it. "Okay."

"Holly—" he took a step toward her "—I just—"

"I've got to get back inside," she said quickly, knowing that if she stayed out here with him one minute longer she'd shatter into thousands of tiny pieces. It took every last ounce of strength she possessed to lean forward and press her lips lightly to his, then smile as she pulled away.

"See you around, Blackwolf," she said with a calm that shocked herself. "Next time you decide to drop in, give me warning. I just might surprise you and bake a cake."

He started to say something, but she didn't—couldn't—give him a chance. She turned, walked away and refused to look back.

Eleven

It felt good to lie under the scorching July sun on a blue-striped chaise lounge beside her Aunt Miranda's pool and sip iced tea. To dip her feet in the cool water every few minutes and leisurely watch the time pass slowly by.

Every hour. Every minute. Every second.

The past seven days had slipped by at the same snail's pace. There had been several trips to the hospital to visit her uncle and she'd had lunch a few times in the town of Red Rock with her aunt, but the rest of Holly's time had mostly been spent staring at endless blue sky.

Since Guy had left seven days, twelve hours and—she glanced at her wristwatch—sixteen minutes ago, she'd been exactly what she'd vowed she'd never be: weepy, maudlin and pathetic.

Just like the old Linda Ronstadt song, "Poor, Poor Pitiful Me."

She'd get over him. She would. Hearts were broken all the time. People survived. They even fell in love again. A little time, a little distance. She'd forget all about him.

In a hundred years or so.

Damn you, Blackwolf.

For the first time in her life, she understood the pain her mother had gone through at Cameron's rejection. But where her mother had chosen a bottle and withdrawal, Holly knew that Guy's leaving would only make her stronger. She would always love him, but she refused to let that love defeat her.

She would have gone home, had told herself that she was anxious to get back to Alaska, but her aunt had asked her to come stay at her house in San Antonio until her uncle got out of the hospital in a few days and Holly hadn't the heart to refuse her. And besides, with Bob and Nicholas covering the store for her, there truly hadn't been a rush to go back.

But in her heart, she knew she was procrastinating, that in some ways, she dreaded going back. There were too many memories of Guy there. Already, she could imagine him sitting at her kitchen table, his baseball cap backward while he ate a slice of pizza, on her sofa watching that silly soap opera, standing at her stove in that frilly apron. Even now, she smiled at that image.

Her smile faded at the image of him lying in her bed beside her, holding her in his arms, making love to her.

The nights would be the hardest, she knew. They would be long and lonely. Empty.

Once again, she cursed him, this time out loud.

"What did you say, dear?"

"I said the sun is a bitch," she said quickly, hoping her aunt would think the flush on her face was from the heat. "You were gone quite a while. How did you do with your errands?"

"Fine." Miranda's gaze dropped. "I ran into an old friend while I was out and we had lunch together."

Holly noticed the blush on her aunt's cheeks and raised a brow. "That old friend wouldn't happen to be Daniel Smythe, would it?"

The color spread on Miranda's face. "Well, yes, actually it was. How did you know?"

Everyone in the family, and most of Red Rock, were talking about Miranda and Daniel. The wealthy oil man had "accidentally" bumped into Miranda and Holly at a restaurant in Red Rock and the sparks flying between the two had been obvious, though Miranda seemed reluctant to admit there was anything going on between them other than a few casual dates.

"Just a guess." Holly sat and reached for the towel on the chaise lounge. "It's hot out here. Why don't we go inside?"

"Holly, dear." Miranda sat on the chaise lounge beside Holly. "There's something I need to talk to you about. I was going to wait until Ryan was out of the hospital, but both your uncle and I decided I should tell you now."

The serious tone of Miranda's voice made Holly

draw in a slow breath. Did they want her gone? Had she done something to upset them? She had stayed longer than she'd planned, but they'd been so insistent, so—

"It's about your inheritance."

She blinked, stunned by the words. *Inheritance?* What inheritance? "I don't know what you're talking about."

"You're a Fortune, Holly," Miranda said firmly. "Your father may not have done right by you, but you're part of this family. Your share of the money left by your grandfather is ten million dollars."

She must have heard wrong. She must have. Still holding the breath she'd sucked in, she blinked twice and simply stared at her aunt. "Ten...*million*...dollars?"

"Yes, dear." Miranda smiled. "Ten million."

"But...but..." Blood rushed to her head. She had to grip the sides of the chaise lounge or she was certain she'd slide right off. "But I'm not really," she sputtered. "I mean, I am, but I'm not even, I mean, my mother wasn't—"

Ten million dollars! She couldn't speak, couldn't even comprehend that much money.

"My brother was your father." Miranda covered Holly's hand with her own. "You belong in this family. I'm only sorry we missed so many precious years."

The sincerity of her words and the tender touch of her hand brought tears to Holly's eyes. "I didn't come here for money," she said around the lump in her throat.

"The money was yours whether you came here or not." Miranda had tears in her eyes, too. "But we so wanted to meet you and welcome you into the family. We're so happy Mr. Blackwolf found you and brought you to us."

Guy. In spite of the bombshell that her aunt had just dropped on her, Holly felt her chest tighten at the mention of his name. As amazing, as wonderful, as *incredible* as Miranda's news was, Holly felt there was something missing, an emptiness without him that no amount of money could ever replace or fill. Emotions welled up inside of her and though she tried, it was impossible to stop the tears.

"Holly, what's wrong?" Her brow furrowed, Miranda slipped an arm around her niece. "This is supposed to be happy news. Have I said something to upset you?"

Miranda's kindness only opened the floodgates wider. Embarrassed by her pitiful outburst, but unable to speak through the steady stream of tears and the thickness in her throat, Holly shook her head, then dropped her face into the towel in her hands and began to sob.

"Oh, sweetheart," Miranda soothed and held her. "Whatever it is, just let it out."

And so she did. She let the years of disappointment wash through her, the hurt and rejection, the pain of lost love. And when finally there wasn't anything left inside her, she rested her head on her aunt's shoulder and felt the warmth and love she'd so desperately missed all her life.

"There now," Miranda murmured as she tucked a

strand of hair behind Holly's ear. "Do you want to tell me about it?"

With a deep sigh, Holly sat, then drew in a long, slow breath. "Yes," she whispered, then cleared her throat as she looked into her aunt's blue eyes. "Yes, I do."

Miranda smiled and took Holly's hand. "Let's go inside out of the sun, dear. We'll have tea and cookies and you can start at the beginning."

Holly nodded, then walked hand in hand with her aunt into the house. She wasn't certain where the beginning was, but something deep inside her told her that this was it.

Guy flew in barely an hour ahead of the summer storm currently pounding Seattle, unloaded his passengers, grabbed his check and headed for home. Two weeks on a private charter with three stuffy executives from a Fortune 500 computer company was enough to drive a man insane. If he never heard the term "B2C" or "value added service" again, it would be three weeks too soon.

Ignoring the rain, he pulled his Jeep Cherokee into his parking spot at his apartment complex, cut the engine, then stepped out of his car directly into a deep puddle. He swore, reached into the back seat and snatched his bag, dropped it, then swore again when half of the contents spilled out onto the wet concrete.

He had to go down on his knees to retrieve a can of shaving cream that rolled under his car, then he scooped up two T-shirts that had also landed in the puddle right beside his brand-new Steve Martini paperback. Muttering fiercely, he stuffed everything back into his bag and stalked toward the stairs leading to his apartment.

He definitely was not having a good day.

But then, he hadn't had even one good day in the past two weeks, he thought sourly. Not since the night he'd left Texas.

Since he'd left Holly.

What an idiot he'd been to think he could just walk out of her life and that would be the end of it. He'd known that he'd miss her, that he'd think about her often. After all they'd been through, of course he'd think about her. And the more he tried *not* to think about her, the more he *did* think about her. Not a waking minute went by that she didn't invade his thoughts. And his dreams. Lord. When he did manage to fall asleep, his dreams about her were hotter than a Texas summer.

What he hadn't considered, what he hadn't expected, was how damn much it would hurt. His insides felt scraped raw, his gut was twisted in knots and his chest felt as if a concrete post had been dropped on him.

He stood in the rain, barely felt the moisture as it seeped through his chambray shirt. As the realization hit him, he might have been standing in a blizzard and he wouldn't have noticed.

He was in love with her.

He stood stock-still in the parking lot, scrubbed a hand over his face, then laughed. Where had *that* come from? He couldn't be in love. He'd never been in love. He didn't know a damn thing about being in love. He was bone-tired, that's all. He'd been flying all over the West Coast with those businessmen for the past two weeks. Maybe he was coming down with something. He felt light-headed, off balance.

Dammit to hell. He *was* in love with her.

Mind-stopping, wildly, moon-eyed *in love with Holly.*

It was one thing to be an idiot, it was another to be completely stupid. *Of course* he was in love with her. He probably had been from the first moment he'd laid eyes on her.

Panic filled him, pounded in his brain.

He'd spent a lifetime never convinced that love truly existed. Lust and physical love, sure. But romantic, hearts and flowers, poetry kind of love? No way.

And now here he stood in a pounding rain, and like a lightning bolt, was struck with the realization that love was not only real, but it also had bit him square on the butt.

Adrenaline rushed through his veins. He turned and splashed through puddles back to his car, jumped in and jammed the key into the ignition. The engine roared to life. He could be in the air in an hour and make it to Texas in maybe four hours. Or jump a commercial flight and be there in three.

He stopped. Was she still in Texas? he wondered? He'd heard from Flynn that her half brother, Jonas, had been arrested for suspicion of poisoning Ryan. But Jonas had been released on bail, and nobody in the family really believed he'd done it.

But Flynn hadn't mentioned Holly, and Guy hadn't had the guts to ask.

So was she back in Alaska then? Back at work, back to her life?

Oh, hell.

He dragged a hand through his wet hair. Who was he kidding? She wouldn't want to see him now. And how could he blame her? He'd walked out on her. She'd been disappointed by every person she'd ever cared about and he was no better than the rest of them. Lord knew, she had plenty of reasons to never even speak to him again.

At least ten million.

He was certain that she'd been told about her inheritance by now. How the hell could he come waltzing back into her life? *Gee, Holly, I know I dropped you like a hot potato, but now that you've got ten million dollars I'm back, and by the way, I really love you.*

Oh, yeah. She'd really believe him.

Dammit, dammit, dammit.

Still swearing, he cut the engine and got out of his car again, slammed the door behind him as he headed back to his apartment.

He'd get drunk, he decided as he trudged up the stairs. A bottle of whiskey would cut the edge and make him forget, if only for a little while, that he lost the first and only woman he'd ever loved because he was a donkey's behind.

He dug his apartment key out of his pocket and opened the door, then froze.

Someone was in his apartment.

The lights were all on, he heard the sound of people talking—the television, he realized, and the most incredible smell was coming from his kitchen.

What the hell?

Cautiously, quietly, he set his bag down and walked slowly toward his kitchen.

Holly.

His heart slammed in his chest. Through the counter opening between the living room and his kitchen, he could only see the top half of her. She stood at his stove, a wooden spoon in her hand as she intently stirred the contents of a frying pan. She wore a chef's white apron over a black tank top. Steam rose from the sauce bubbling in the frying pan.

"Holly?"

She glanced up at sound of his voice and smiled. "Hi. You're just in time. This will be—heavens! You're dripping wet!"

"Huh?" He glanced down at his clothes, realized his shirt and jeans were soaked through. "It's raining."

Now *that* was certainly smooth. The woman he'd been fantasizing about, the woman he'd just now realized that he desperately loved, the woman he thought he'd never see again, suddenly turns up in his kitchen and he gives her a weather report.

"Is it?" She turned her attention back to the stove. "Well, why don't you change your clothes? Dinner's almost ready."

He actually started to say okay, even started to turn, then shook his head to clear the fog that seemed to have rolled into his brain.

He swallowed hard, cleared his throat. A mere six feet and a kitchen counter was all that separated them and it was all he could do not to leap at her and drag her into his arms. But confusion, not to mention fear that this was not what he hoped it was, kept him rooted to where he stood.

"Holly," he asked carefully, "what are you doing here?"

The spoon paused, then she continued stirring. "I'm making you dinner, what's it look like? I hope you like linguine and clams in an artichoke and red roasted pepper sauce."

He shook his head. "That's not what I mean. I mean what are you—" He stopped, eyed her with suspicion. "You're cooking?"

She shrugged one smooth, bare shoulder. "Nothing too fancy. I'm a little out of practice. Would you like a cheese pastry puff before you change?"

Hope, just a glimmer, had him releasing the breath he'd been holding. He took a step toward her, kept his gaze leveled with hers. "I thought you said you couldn't cook."

"No, I said I *didn't* cook." She took a taste of the sauce, furrowed her brow, then reached for the salt shaker. "Big difference. No, you don't." She pointed the spoon in her hand at him when he took another step toward her. "Out of the kitchen. We saw what happened the last time you got too close to an oven."

Holly also knew what would happen if he got too close to *her*. Her knees would buckle for sure and she'd throw herself in his arms. As it was, her heart was pounding so hard she was certain he could hear.

If she was going to get through this, she needed him to keep his distance. She was putting herself out on the edge as far as she could possibly go. If he came around that corner, if he touched her, she'd crumble.

When he stopped, she mentally breathed a deep sigh of relief. Desperately she needed to not only keep the conversation light, but to keep it going, if only for a few more moments.

"I hope you don't mind that I asked Flynn to call your office for me this morning to find out when you'd be coming home." She knew she was rambling now, but she didn't care. "Oh, and I also told your apartment manager, Mr. Wendall, that I was your sister visiting from Texas and that you said it was all right to let me in. He's such a nice man."

"Mrs. Wendall," Guy said as he slid onto a bar stool, "thought the same thing until she caught him in the laundry room helping Mrs. Potter from 12A fold her clothes."

In spite of her racing pulse, Holly glanced up in surprise. "What's wrong with that?"

"Well, it seems he'd just taken those clothes off the woman, if you catch my drift."

"Mr. Wendall?" She tried to imagine the semibald man who looked more like a roly-poly bug than a seducer, getting frisky in the laundry room. "Wonders never cease."

"Which brings us back to you being here."

Once again, Guy turned his intense wolf-gray eyes on her. Holly's heart jumped into her throat.

"I was in the neighborhood?"

He lifted a brow.

She sucked in a breath. "I...I—" *Love you.* But the two little words caught in her throat right next to her heart. She swallowed hard. "I—"

The timer went off on the oven.

She ignored it.

If she was going to do this, it had to be now.

Still, she didn't move.

His gaze stayed on hers as he started to rise from the bar stool. "You, ah, want me to get that?"

"No!" She put out a hand to stop him. "Stay where you are."

Both brows came up now, but he eased back down.

Panic gripped her. This was a bad idea. A bad, bad idea. What *had* she been thinking when she'd planned this?

But it was too late to back out now. And even if she could, she knew in her heart that she wouldn't, that she didn't want to. And if it made her the biggest fool that ever lived, then so be it.

She sucked in a deep breath, held it, and turned toward the oven to shut off the timer.

"My God!"

Behind her, Holly heard the crash. She whirled, gasped at the sight of Guy on the floor, spread across the kitchen doorway, his legs caught in the bar stool he'd just fallen off of.

"Guy!" She hurried to him and bent down beside him. "Are you all right?"

"*What* are you wearing?" He stared hard at her as he struggled to sit. "Definitely not a tank top."

"It's a teddy." Her cheeks burning, she tugged at

her apron in an attempt to cover the black lace lingerie she had on. "I—I thought you might like it."

"*Like* it?" Eyes wide, he fell back on the floor again. "Good Lord, woman, are you trying to give me a heart attack?"

The burning on her cheeks spread to her face and down her neck. What had possessed her to put on high heels and a black teddy under an apron and surprise him like this? she thought in despair. But she knew the answer to that.

Love. Love turned a person inside out and upside down and definitely made them think and do foolish things.

And she was the biggest fool of all.

When he started to laugh, she narrowed her eyes and pressed her lips tightly together. "What's so funny?"

"You—you...came here," he managed to say between laughs. "To me."

That did it. It was one thing to reject her, quite another to make fun of her. She'd bared herself to him, body and soul, not only to prove to him how much she loved him, but because she'd been so certain that he loved her back. Well, if he didn't love her, and he didn't want her, then fine.

"Listen up, Blackwolf." She stood, hands on her waist, too angry to care that she was nearly naked under this silly apron. "This was obviously a mistake. A big one. I flew halfway across the country, bought this ridiculous piece of fluff and *cooked* for you, buster." When he started to rise, she dug a heel in his chest and shoved him back down. "The next time

I fall in love, I'll make sure it's not with an egotistical, arrogant, self-serving son of a—''

She hadn't known that a person could move so fast. One minute she was standing over him, letting him have it, the next thing she knew she was on the floor underneath him.

"God, you're beautiful when you're mad.'' When she tried to slug him, he grabbed her hands and pinned them to her sides. "Kiss me.''

"Like hell I will.'' She wiggled under him, but the close contact of their bodies only aroused her, so she went still. "You're all wet. Get off me, you jerk.''

"I thought you loved me,'' he murmured and brought his face close to hers.

"No, I don't.''

"But you just said you did.''

There was amusement in his eyes, which only infuriated her all the more. She struggled once again, almost desperate to escape him now before she begged him to take her, right here, right now, dignity be damned. "Well, I don't love you anymore, so get off me.''

"You love me, all right. You just said you did and I won't let you take it back.''

She went still. "You won't?''

"Not a chance.''

Hope soared. Made her blood race and her breath catch. Made her forget that his rain-drenched clothes were now soaking through her apron. She raised her eyes to his, saw something there she hadn't seen before. Prayed that it wasn't just what she wanted so desperately for it to be.

"Nothing, no one like you, has ever come into my life before," Guy said quietly. "I never believed that anyone would, that it was even possible. I think I must have known that first day, in Doc's office, when I opened my eyes and you stared back at me. But I was too cynical, too afraid, to believe it."

"Just say it, Blackwolf," Holly said tightly, afraid that she was going to be the one to have a heart attack if he didn't hurry. "For God's sake, just *say it.*"

"I'm crazy about you." He lightly pressed a kiss to her nose, then smiled softly down at her. "I love you."

Relief poured through her, warmed the chill that had settled into her limbs and her heart. "You love me?"

"Yeah." He kissed one cheek, then the other. "I do."

Holly thrilled at his words and when he kissed her, a gentle melting of lips and hearts, she felt a tear slide from the corner of her eye. No one had ever kissed her like this, with such tenderness. With such love.

When he pulled away, then brought her hands to his mouth and kissed her fingers, Holly blinked at the moisture in her eyes.

"I would have come after you," he said as he stared into her eyes. "I don't give a damn about the money. All that matters to me is you, Holly. Being with you."

"Is that why you left?" she asked in amazement. "Because you knew about the money?"

"I know it was stupid." He sucked in a breath. "It just spooked me. My God, ten million dollars. I was afraid you'd think I stayed because of it. That you'd always have doubts. But I'll sign a prenuptial if you want,'' he rushed on. "I just need you to know, to be certain that—''

She put her hand over his mouth. Wide-eyed, she stared at him. "Did you say prenuptial?''

He nodded, but with her hand still covering his mouth, he stayed quiet.

"Guy Blackwolf,'' she said breathlessly, "are you asking me to *marry* you?''

He nodded again, then gently tugged her hand away. "Will you, Holly?'' he whispered. "Will you please marry me?''

Would she marry him? Dazed, her mind reeling, she had to wait for oxygen to return to her lungs before she could speak.

Laughing, she threw her arms around his neck and dragged him closer. "You big idiot, of *course* I'll marry you.''

He gave a whoop, then kissed her long and hard, until her body and bones and mind turned to the consistency of warm taffy. It was a kiss that spoke of love and caring, of forever.

When he drew back, she slowly opened her eyes.

"Holly,'' he asked, "what made you decide to come here?''

"Miranda,'' she said softly. "She told me that if I loved you, I should never let you go, no matter what the cost. I could see in her eyes that there was someone in her past, someone she'd loved and lost. She was so sad, Guy. Looking at her, I knew that if I didn't at least try, if I didn't come here, that I'd have that same look, feel that same emptiness for the rest of my life.''

She took his face in her hands. ''I don't care about the money, either, Guy. Not without you. But I will be able to help the school in Twin Pines and get my store back on its feet, as well.'' She smiled at him. ''I just might buy you a new plane, too.''

''My insurance company will take care of that, thank you very much. But I was thinking that I could set up a base in Twin Pines and fly the day shifts and short runs for the outback regions. Keegan was the one who first suggested it.''

She looked at him in disbelief. ''Keegan suggested that?''

Guy smiled. ''He'll probably kick himself for giving me the idea, but then, he's going to have to get used to me being around permanently. Between tourists and shipping runs for locals, I just might make a good enough living to support a wife and, oh say, three or four kids?''

Three or four? Her throat thickened and she could barely whisper, ''You want children?''

He nodded. ''Ever since I saw you with all those kids, reading that silly story about a zebra, I couldn't stop wondering what it would be like, how it would feel, to have a son or daughter of my own, *our* son or daughter.'' He hesitated, then furrowed his brow at the sight of tears in her eyes. ''You want them, don't you? If you don't, it's all right. I love you and if—''

She reached up and dragged his mouth to hers, poured her love into the kiss. She had everything now, the family she'd missed and the man she loved. If this was a dream, she never wanted it to end.

"Yes, yes, yes," she murmured, her lips still on his. "I want it all, Blackwolf. You, babies, a house. Everything."

At the sound of a man's familiar voice coming from the living room, Guy lifted his head and frowned. "Is that Gerald's voice I hear, from *Storm's Cove?*"

Holly grinned. "I taped the past two weeks' episodes for you, just in case you missed any."

He chuckled softly. "I'm going to be too busy to watch them for a while." He slid a hand up her bare leg. "Lord, woman, have you any idea what you do to me?"

She sucked in a breath when his hand moved up her thigh. "Only what I want to do to you," she said, amazed at the dexterity of his fingers when he found the snaps of her teddy.

At the faint smell of something burning, her eyes flew open.

"Oh, no!" She rolled away from him and flew into the kitchen. "Dessert!"

"You made dessert, too? Damn, but I'm one hell of a lucky guy." Grinning like a fool, he rose and followed her into the kitchen, watched as she grabbed a set of hot pads, then whisked her creation from the oven and set it on the stovetop. It looked like a fluffy cream pie, slightly charred on the top.

Baked Alaska.

He started to laugh, then scooped her into his arms

and hugged her close. She laughed, too, wound her arms around his neck.

"Dinner's ready," she said breathlessly between kisses.

"Later." He carried her out of the kitchen, into his bedroom.

And it was. Much, much later.

*　*　*　*　*

*Is Jonas Goodfellow guilty
of poisoning Ryan Fortune?
Tara Summers would say that
the only crime her boss has committed
is a crime of passion!
Be sure to watch for*

HER BOSS'S BABY,

*coming only to Silhouette Desire
in October 2001.*

*And now, for a sneak preview,
please turn the page.*

One

"Thanks for coming," Jonas Goodfellow said to Tara as the door to his cell swung open. "You're certainly a sight for sore eyes."

Though he resisted the urge to give his assistant an appreciative hug in front of such an audience of thugs, she was not given to such reserve. Wrapping her arms about him, Tara Summers brushed a kiss across his stubbled cheek thus causing yet another crude comment to bubble up from the gutter of another captive's low mind.

For all the times Jonas had imagined holding this woman in his arms, he couldn't believe how good she felt. Way too good. For the hundredth time, he had to remind himself that theirs was an employee/employer relationship. Friendly and respectful. Anything more would be taking advantage of Tara's sweet nature and naiveté.

"Let's get you out of here," she whispered in his ear.

The sensation of her breath upon his neck caused Jonas's skin to tingle. What was that scent she was wearing? A heady mixture of flowers and musk, it was an importer's dream. Jonas was certain he could sell gallons of the stuff to other men just as susceptible as he to sensual delight.

After two days of confinement, he was eager to leave the premises. Jonas said a little prayer of thanksgiving as he entered the light of freedom. Relative freedom, he amended, cursing the fact that for the time being the bail money Tara had procured from the business liberated him only from his cell. Unless the charges against him were dropped, Jonas would be required to remain in the tightly knit community of Red Rock until the time of his trial. As far as he could tell, the small town existed for the sole purpose of servicing the Fortune family—that nest of vipers he had so foolishly hoped would welcome him as kith and kin.

"I can't begin to tell you how much I appreciate your coming to bail me out," he began stiffly.

Knowing how Jonas hated to be indebted to anyone, Tara would have none of it. "You'd do the same for me," she assured him with a blinding smile. "In fact, I believe you already have."

"It's hardly the same," he retorted bitterly.

"Of course it is," she insisted. "It's my turn to take care of you now."

Though Jonas looked genuinely insulted by the thought, Tara felt certain his masculine pride would ultimately take a back seat to his gratitude. At least she hoped so as she directed him toward the car she had rented for the length of their stay in Red Rock.

Feminine instinct compelled her to toss him the keys. Having worked so closely with this man for the past five years, she had absolutely no fear that he would do anything so foolish as attempting to bolt from town. She smiled at him as he opened the car door. Even under the most dire of circumstances, she could always count on Jonas to play the part of a gentleman. It was one of the things she found most endearing about him.

Tara filled him in on the arrangements she had made as they drove to the hotel where they would be staying until this whole mess was cleared up. A blush crept up her neckline as she explained in a rush how two separate bedrooms adjoined a relatively spacious central living area that would have to serve as their temporary office "until this little matter gets cleared up."

"Always the master of understatement," Jonas quipped, pulling up in front of the hotel.

As grateful as he was that Tara had taken all the necessary precautions to keep his mind off the gravity of the situation, it bothered Jonas that she seemed so unsettled by the thought of sharing close quarters with him.

Switching off the ignition, he leaned across the seat. Tipping her chin up to force her to make direct eye contact with him, he asked her point-blank,

"What are you afraid of? Haven't I always behaved like a perfect gentleman?"

Remembering some of the late nights they had spent working overtime when she had caught him looking at her as more than a mere employee, Tara wanted to say *That is the problem! What I'm really afraid of is that you have absolutely no interest in me as a woman. A woman who wants to be more than just a loyal employee.*

Brazenly she traced the outline of his jaw with her index finger. If anything, she thought that two-day stubble and haunted look in his eyes made him more outrageously masculine than ever. Indeed, such a rebel could capture any woman's heart with a single glance.

"Has it ever occurred to you that maybe you're the one who has something to fear?" Tara squeaked out, in a voice that she barely recognized as her own.

The sound of Jonas's laughter filled the car with its deep base tones. Putting her hand demurely back in her own lap, he threw in one of his patented winks with hopes of keeping the mood light.

"Just in case you're tempted to play with fire, I promise to keep *my* door locked. I'm already in enough trouble without being accused of robbing the cradle."

FORTUNES OF TEXAS: THE LOST HEIRS
Fortune Family Tree

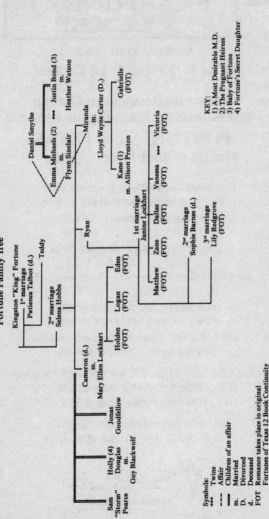

KEY:
1) A Most Desirable M.D.
2) The Pregnant Heiress
3) Baby of Fortune
4) Fortune's Secret Daughter

Symbols:
*** Twins
--- Affair
 — Children of an affair
m. Married
D. Divorced
d. Deceased
FOT Romance takes place in original
Fortunes of Texas 12 Book Continuity

SILHOUETTE®
MAKES YOU
A STAR!

Feel like a star with Silhouette.

We will fly you and a guest to New York City for an exciting weekend stay at a glamorous 5-star hotel. Experience a refreshing day at one of New York's trendiest spas and have your photo taken by a professional. Plus, receive $1,000 U.S. spending money!

Flowers...long walks...dinner for two... how does Silhouette Books make romance come alive for you?

Send us a script, with 500 words or less, along with visuals (only drawings, magazine cutouts or photographs or combination thereof). Show us how Silhouette Makes Your Love Come Alive. Be creative and have fun. No purchase necessary. All entries must be clearly marked with your name, address and telephone number. All entries will become property of Silhouette and are not returnable. **Contest closes September 28, 2001.**

Please send your entry to: **Silhouette Makes You a Star!**

In U.S.A.
P.O. Box 9069
Buffalo, NY, 14269-9069

In Canada
P.O. Box 637
Fort Erie, ON, L2A 5X3

Look for contest details on the next page, by visiting www.eHarlequin.com or request a copy by sending a self-addressed envelope to the applicable address above. Contest open to Canadian and U.S. residents who are 18 or over. Void where prohibited.

Silhouette®
Where love comes alive™

Our lucky winner's photo will appear in a Silhouette ad. Join the fun!

SRMYAS1

HARLEQUIN "SILHOUETTE MAKES YOU A STAR!" CONTEST 1308
OFFICIAL RULES
NO PURCHASE NECESSARY TO ENTER

1. To enter, follow directions published in the offer to which you are responding. Contest begins June 1, 2001, and ends on September 28, 2001. Entries must be postmarked by September 28, 2001, and received by October 5, 2001. Enter by hand-printing (or typing) on an 8 ½" x 11" piece of paper your name, address (including zip code), contest number/name and attaching a script containing 500 words or less, along with drawings, photographs or magazine cutouts, or combinations thereof (i.e., collage) on no larger than 9" x 12" piece of paper, describing how the Silhouette books make romance come alive for you. Mail via first-class mail to: Harlequin "Silhouette Makes You a Star!" Contest 1308, (in the U.S.) P.O. Box 9069, Buffalo, NY 14269-9069, (in Canada) P.O. Box 637, Fort Erie, Ontario, Canada L2A 5X3. Limit one entry per person, household or organization.

2. Contests will be judged by a panel of members of the Harlequin editorial, marketing and public relations staff. Fifty percent of criteria will be judged against script and fifty percent will be judged against drawing, photographs and/or magazine cutouts. Judging criteria will be based on the following:

   - Sincerity—25%
   - Originality and Creativity—50%
   - Emotionally Compelling—25%

   In the event of a tie, duplicate prizes will be awarded. Decisions of the judges are final.

3. All entries become the property of Torstar Corp. and may be used for future promotional purposes. Entries will not be returned. No responsibility is assumed for lost, late, illegible, incomplete, inaccurate, nondelivered or misdirected mail.

4. Contest open only to residents of the U.S. (except Puerto Rico) and Canada who are 18 years of age or older, and is void wherever prohibited by law; all applicable laws and regulations apply. Any litigation within the Province of Quebec respecting the conduct or organization of a publicity contest may be submitted to the Régie des alcools, des courses et des jeux for a ruling. Any litigation respecting the awarding of a prize may be submitted to the Régie des alcools, des courses et des jeux only for the purpose of helping the parties reach a settlement. Employees and immediate family members of Torstar Corp. and D. L. Blair, Inc., their affiliates, subsidiaries and all other agencies, entities and persons connected with the use, marketing or conduct of this contest are not eligible to enter. Taxes on prizes are the sole responsibility of the winner. Acceptance of any prize offered constitutes permission to use winner's name, photograph or other likeness for the purposes of advertising, trade and promotion on behalf of Torstar Corp., its affiliates and subsidiaries without further compensation to the winner, unless prohibited by law.

5. Winner will be determined no later than November 30, 2001, and will be notified by mail. Winner will be required to sign and return an Affidavit of Eligibility/Release of Liability/Publicity Release form within 15 days after winner notification. Noncompliance within that time period may result in disqualification and an alternative winner may be selected. All travelers must execute a Release of Liability prior to ticketing and must possess required travel documents (e.g., passport, photo ID) where applicable. Trip must be booked by December 31, 2001, and completed within one year of notification. No substitution of prize permitted by winner. Torstar Corp. and D. L. Blair, Inc., their parents, affiliates and subsidiaries are not responsible for errors in printing of contest, entries and/or game pieces. In the event of printing or other errors that may result in unintended prize values or duplication of prizes, all affected game pieces or entries shall be null and void. **Purchase or acceptance of a product offer does not improve your chances of winning.**

6. Prizes: (1) Grand Prize—A 2-night/3-day trip for two (2) to New York City, including round-trip coach air transportation nearest winner's home and hotel accommodations (double occupancy) at The Plaza Hotel, a glamorous afternoon makeover at a trendy New York spa, $1,000 in U.S. spending money and an opportunity to have a professional photo taken and appear in a Silhouette advertisement (approximate retail value: $7,000). (10) Ten Runner-Up Prizes of gift packages (retail value $50 ea.). Prizes consist of only those items listed as part of the prize. Limit one prize per person. Prize is valued in U.S. currency.

7. For the name of the winner (available after December 31, 2001) send a self-addressed, stamped envelope to: Harlequin "Silhouette Makes You a Star!" Contest 1197 Winners, P.O. Box 4200 Blair, NE 68009-4200 or you may access the www.eHarlequin.com Web site through February 28, 2002.

Contest sponsored by Torstar Corp., P.O. Box 9042, Buffalo, NY 14269-9042.

SRMYAS2